D1076315

Max settled Phoebe between his knees, her back tucked against his front.

The cellar wasn't huge, but Max didn't expect to be there for long as the fire was moving so fast. The only question was, would they still be here after it had roared through?

The lack of space meant they couldn't sit face to face, and for that Max was grateful as he knew he'd find his growing awareness of one very womanly woman too distracting. Phoebe was strong and brave and warm and vulnerable, all at once. And he'd never met anyone like her.

The wind increased in intensity as they waited. The roof timbers creaked and groaned under the roar of the fire. The flames would be leaping from treetop to treetop, threatening to devour the house. And them along with it. If the fire took hold they didn't stand a chance.

Phoebe half turned towards Max and buried her face in his shoulder. Involuntarily he wrapped her in his arms, silently offering comfort. She felt good nestled against him, head tucked to one side. She was a perfect fit.

Suddenly the house gave an almighty shudder, and then lay silent. Had the impossible happened? Had they escaped?

Dear Reader

Every woman loves a Mills & Boon® romance—and who could resist a firefighter as a hero? We certainly couldn't. So when gorgeous firefighter Max Williams strolled onto the page, we didn't even try to resist giving him his own story.

More importantly, our paramedic heroine Phoebe didn't stand a chance against Max's charms when he sauntered into her life, arriving to run the local country fire station in the middle of a burning hot Australian summer.

Max and Phoebe's story is set in South Australia, in the Adelaide Hills: hills that are covered in dense bush, with quaint little towns nestled into the valleys. Summers there are extremely hot; the bush turns tinderbox brown, water is scarce, and bushfires pose an ever-present danger, pitting people against the elements. This battle happens all over our vast continent—not surprising since in places it's no less wild or dangerous than when European settlers first arrived 230 years ago. What is amazing is that Mills & Boon has existed for 100 of those 230 years. It's an incredible achievement, and we are thrilled to be part of the Mills and Boon success story—a success that has made it possible for us to reach readers around the world.

EMERGENCY: WIFE NEEDED is the first book in a two-book series. We had so much fun with Max and Phoebe, we couldn't say goodbye. Luckily, Ned Kellaway, Max's firefighter buddy, proved irresistible, and his story will be on sale early next year.

Our editor fell in love with Max, and we hope you do, too. So here's to Max, and to all our readers, and here's to Mills & Boon Medical™ Romances sweeping women everywhere off their feet for the next hundred years and beyond.

Love

Emily Forbes

EMERGENCY: WIFE NEEDED

BY
EMILY FORBES

MILLS & BOON®

Pure reading pleasure™

First published in Great Britain 2008
Large Print edition 2009
Harlequin Mills & Boon Limited,
Eton House, 18-24 Paradise Road,
Richmond, Surrey TW9 1SR

© Emily Forbes 2008

ISBN: 978 0 263 20487 2

Set in Times Roman 16¼ on 19 pt.
17-0109-55927

Printed and bound in Great Britain
by CPI Antony Rowe, Chippenham, Wiltshire

Emily Forbes is the pseudonym of two sisters who share both a passion for writing and a life-long love of reading. Beyond books and their families, their interests include cooking (food is a recurring theme in their books!), learning languages, playing the piano and netball, as well as an addiction to travel—armchair is fine, but anything involving a plane ticket is better. Home for both is South Australia, where they live three minutes apart with their husbands and four young children. With backgrounds in business administration, law, arts, clinical psychology and physiotherapy, they have worked in many areas. This past professional experience adds to their writing in many ways: legal dilemmas, psychological ordeals and business scandals are all intermeshed with the medical settings of their stories. And, since nothing could ever be as delicious as spending their days telling the stories of gorgeous heroes and spirited heroines, they are eternally grateful their mutual dream of writing for a living came true. They would love you to visit and keep up to date with current news and future releases at the Medical™ Romance authors' website: http://www.medicalromance.com

Recent titles by the same author:

WEDDING AT PELICAN BEACH
THE SURGEON'S LONGED-FOR BRIDE
A MOTHER IN THE MAKING
EMERGENCY AT PELICAN BEACH

This book would not have been possible
without Glen, AKA Cookie,
our real-life firefighter, whose
fabulous inside information was
only surpassed by his ability to slide down
that pole with such panache.

Thanks also to Tim,
the dashing lead singer from the
Dirty Strangers, for providing the
inspiration for our rock god hero,
and to James, for playing the role of
our personal publicity guru
with natural flair.

This one's for the boys!

CHAPTER ONE

PHOEBE WILSON parked the ambulance at the intersection of the Hahndorf and Woodside roads, overlooking an almost dry riverbed, as her partner sent a message back to the station, advising they were in position.

The wind howled around the ambulance, carrying with it the sound of sirens as other units were dispatched from the stations throughout the Hills area. A red glow lit the horizon to the north where the fire service crews were trying to subdue the raging beast that was the bushfire. The fires, already burning for almost twenty-four hours, were steadily consuming the land lying between them and Hahndorf. The forecast maximum temperature for today was a blistering forty degrees and the angry north wind, combined with tinderbox conditions following one of the driest winters on record, made perfect conditions for fuelling bushfires.

The knowledge made calm acceptance of their instructions to sit and wait difficult. Yet here they were. Sitting. Waiting. Both of which were a stock-standard part of the job, although not so easy today.

They were on one periphery of the bushfire, the first in line to treat any casualties the fire crews might bring out to them. In theory, Phoebe and her partner were on their days off but all emergency personnel had been called in. The bushfires were threatening homes and lives and it was all hands on deck. Or at least all hands ready and waiting to be on deck. Phoebe searched for her Discman as her partner, Steve, organised his newspapers. As usual he'd brought the form guide for the horse races and *The Trading Post* along to help kill time.

'What are you looking for this week?' Phoebe asked, nodding at *The Trading Post*.

'Old clocks for Dutchy to restore while he's out of action.'

'How's he doing?' she asked, enquiring after a collegue. 'Have you spoken to him lately?'

'He's OK. His ankle's feeling good, the pins seem to be holding it all together. He's still peeved about the accident happening in the first place, especially as he's the health and safety rep for the fire crews.'

'But it's not like he was the one who slid down the pole wet.' Phoebe suppressed a laugh. The accident hadn't been funny but the mental image she got whenever she thought about it was. A firefighter shooting down a wet pole at high speed was like a slapstick cartoon. 'He didn't know Tiny had been stupid enough to slide down when he was wet.'

'No, but it was an accident that could have been avoided.'

'Most of them are.'

'Yeah, I guess. Have you seen the new signs at the top of the pole now?'

Phoebe nodded. The new signs instructed the emergency personnel to use the stairs, *not* the pole, if they were wet.

'I still can't believe the loss of traction created enough force in a one-storey slide to fracture his ankle.'

'Unless you can slow yourself down using one

foot as a brake, you slide down pretty fast. Dutchy's got a fair bit of weight behind him—it's like trying to stop a freight train. He probably hit the floor at an awkward angle and his ankle couldn't take the pressure.'

'His replacement should be here tomorrow. Max Williams?'

'That's what I've heard.'

'Let's hope he fits in all right. It'll make it tough otherwise—we're such a tightly knit unit.'

She glanced out of the window as Steve buried his nose in his papers. The strong north wind was carrying fingernail-sized particles of ash to them and she watched as they drifted around the ambulance. Despite the mask, which covered the lower half of her face, the smell of the burning bush filled her nose. She didn't know what made her more nervous, sitting in a stationary ambulance on the edge of a bushfire, shrouded in thick brown smoke, or having a French test looming tomorrow.

She was less prepared for the second event, woefully prepared. Pulling a face, she plugged the headphones into her Discman and slipped them into her ears. It looked like any last-minute swotting would have to be done now.

'What's with the long face?' Steve laughed as he looked up from the paper. 'Aren't your endless courses meant to be your downtime? Your fun?'

Stretching her legs as much as the cramped confines of the front of the ambulance would allow, she simultaneously poked him in the ribs. 'I've got a test tomorrow and this time I want to blitz it.'

'After you bombed out in the last one, Little Miss Competitive?'

Turning up her nose, Phoebe ignored him and waved a hand at the smoke billowing across the bush in front of them. 'I'm not sure if my lecturer will accept a bushfire for an excuse. He's already decided I'm a lousy student.'

'Are you?'

'Afraid so, so bug off and let me cram.' She hit the play button and tried to tune out Steve's attempts to distract her by counting to ten in French. Again and again. At least she'd remember her numbers tomorrow. Maybe.

She parroted back the phrases which she'd hoped by now would be familiar but which for some reason had decided to jumble in her brain, and while she recited she watched, almost mesmerised, as the dark smoke danced and swirled, the wind tugging the air and giving it a life of its own. Even within the close confines of the ambulance she could taste the smoke. It coated her tongue and any time she drank from her water bottle to wet her throat, the taste was tainted by the odour of the smoke. The sun was a hazy orange ball hanging in the sky, obscured by the smoke. It was almost midday yet the light suggested it was much later in the afternoon.

Phoebe tried to concentrate on her French. The man on the disc was conjugating verbs and she realised she was supposed to be repeating the words in the pauses. She could listen to a French accent for ever without tiring of it. Today it had the added bonus of blocking out the noise of the fire, but if she didn't concentrate she'd never pass tomorrow night's test. Since joining the ambulance service a little over a year ago she'd become skilled at making the most of her idle time, something she hadn't had much experience with in her past life. Then every minute had been accounted for and she'd been permanently stretched to her limits. She increased the volume and began repeating the words.

She glanced out her window again as she

muttered to herself. A few feet to her left a second ambulance was parked. She could see Bluey lying back, eyes closed, as he catnapped while Ken read. Everyone had their own way of killing time. Looking back towards the river, she thought the smoke was getting thicker. It was almost a solid wall and the lights of the emergency vehicles bounced off it, reflecting red and orange, mimicking the flames. Her heart rate increased as she imagined the fire heading in her direction. This wasn't the first bushfire she'd attended but it was, by far, the most formidable and she closed her eyes as she tried to get her imagination under control.

Steve nudged her in the side, attracting her attention. His hand was on the volume control for the two-way radio and she removed her headphones to listen to him.

'Pete Brady's been injured. The firies are bringing him out to us.'

The Onkaparinga River in front of her formed the south boundary of the Bradys' farm. Their house and most of the sheds were less than five kilometres from where the ambulances were parked and she wondered again just how close the fire was. Apparently the firefighters had burnt a fire break on the other side of the river but the smoke was now so dense she couldn't see that far. All she could hope was that the break was large enough to stop the fire, but she doubted it. She couldn't imagine that a fire that burned with such fierce intensity would hesitate at this pitiful excuse of a river and give up the fight.

A red Metropolitan Fire Service car emerged from the smoke, its headlights and rooftop emergency lights piercing the gloom as it drew up alongside the ambulances. Phoebe and Steve took a quick gulp of water before repositioning their face masks and scrambling from their vehicle, ready to assist.

The fireman had his door open and was already helping Pete from the car. Pete leant heavily on the other man and hobbled the few steps across to Phoebe. She quickly moved to Pete's right side, taking some of his weight. The firefighter nodded at her in acknowledgment and she felt a flicker of recognition as she met his gaze.

She turned away, concentrating on getting Pete safely to the ambulance, focussing on her job. It was unlike her to be easily distracted yet she couldn't help risking another glance.

He wasn't familiar, she was sure she'd never met him before, so why did she feel like she had?

He was tall, at least six feet two inches. She was nearly five feet ten herself and he was definitely several inches taller. His thick, dark brown hair curled slightly over his ears and at his neck and was currently covered with a layer of soot. Goggles were hanging around his neck, drawing her eyes to his well-defined jaw, but it was his eyes, so dark they were almost black, that had sent the shiver of familiarity through her.

Pete stumbled, catching his foot on a small rock, and Phoebe and the fireman both tightened their hold on him. The fireman flashed a smile at Phoebe, his teeth startlingly white and perfect, and she caught her breath and almost stumbled herself.

What was it about this man that affected her like this?

She let out the breath she'd been holding and tore her gaze away as Steve asked a question.

'What happened?'

'We found Pete just outside one of his sheds. He'd fallen into a rabbit hole and twisted his knee. He'd dragged himself to the shed. He's suffering from smoke inhalation as well.' His voice was deep and he spoke with a South Australian accent, his vowels more rounded and English-sounding in comparison to her own east coast Aussie twang.

'Thanks. We've got it from here.' Bluey took over and got Pete settled on a stretcher before pushing it into the ambulance.

'What's it like out there?' Steve asked.

Out of the corner of her eye Phoebe could see Bluey hooking Pete up to the oxygen and a saline drip but her attention had again drifted to the fire-fighter and she couldn't seem to tear herself away.

'Not good. The fire's several kilometres wide and this wind's not helping. We haven't got it under control but it hasn't broken the containment lines.'

From his erect posture to the carriage of his head through to his strong voice, he exuded confidence. In fact, since he'd arrived on the scene she hadn't worried about the fire. Everything seemed more controlled now.

'I'll leave you to it, then.' He nodded at them both before turning back to the MFS car. As he walked away Phoebe realised she didn't know his name and then wondered why that mattered. She had other things to worry about. She hopped into the ambulance and began to examine Pete's knee.

'Anyone know if Kerry and the girls got out OK?' Pete was asking after his family.

'We haven't heard of any problems but I'll check on that for you,' Steve replied. 'Would they have reported in at the police station?'

'They should have—that's always the plan.'

'No worries, then. I'll find out.'

Phoebe ran her hands over Pete's knee. It was quite swollen and tender on palpation over the medial aspect and seemed quite unstable when she tested the cruciate ligament, but he didn't complain of pain with that test.

'Looks like you've done some ligament damage, probably involving your cartilage, too, and I suspect your anterior cruciate ligament is ruptured.'

'That went a long time ago,' Pete said. 'An old football injury. But the pain on this side is new.'

'I reckon you'll live but you won't be fighting any more fires today.'

'What about the house?'

'The MFS and the CFS are there, you'll just have to trust them to do their jobs. We need to get you back to town,' Phoebe said as she wrapped an icepack around his knee before checking his oxygen sats.

'Kerry and the girls are fine.' Steve reported. 'Kerry'll meet you at the hospital. Ken and Bluey will take you in—they're due for a break.'

The two-way radio crackled into life as Phoebe tightened the straps to secure Pete to the stretcher. Steve took the call, interrupting Phoebe. 'We gotta go. Bill Chappell's had a suspected heart attack.' She raced back to the other ambulance, jumping into the passenger seat as Steve turned around, heading up the hill, heading into the smoke and towards the fire.

'Where is he?'

'Still at home. We can get through past Pete's place.' The reduced visibility hindered their speed and Steve turned the siren on to alert any other vehicles to their presence.

Once again, Phoebe was aware of her heart rate increasing with every metre they advanced towards the fire. She knew from the emergency services controllers that they weren't in any immediate danger yet the conditions were making her nervous. She took a deep breath but that only made matters worse as she got a lungful of smoke-tainted air. She took another long drink of water and tried mentally reciting her French verbs. As a distraction technique it was quite successful and she was just beginning her second run-through when Steve turned into Bill's driveway.

Maureen Chappell met them at the front door and gave them a quick summary of Bill's medical history as they made their way to the lounge room where their patient was slumped in a chair. His breathing was shallow, his complexion grey and his skin was coated with a sheen of perspiration—in short, he didn't look the picture of health.

Maureen had told them Bill was complaining of left chest pain, extending down his left arm. Phoebe administered a quick dose of GTN spray under Bill's tongue while Steve recorded his obs.

Phoebe unbuttoned Bill's shirt and applied the sticky electrodes for the portable ECG machine as Steve ran an oxygen line to the mask he placed over Bill's mouth and nose. Together they set up a saline drip and while Steve waited to see if Bill's condition stabilized, Phoebe returned to the ambulance to fetch the stretcher. Bill had suffered episodes of angina in the past and the safest place for him at the moment was in hospital.

The return trip to Hahndorf, with Phoebe driving, took less than twenty minutes but in that time several fire engines passed them on the road as they headed out to the fires. Each time one passed by Phoebe found herself looking into the trucks, looking for a glimpse of the unknown fireman.

After delivering Bill into the care of the nurses at the hospital, Phoebe and Steve returned to the station for their scheduled break. The combined fire and ambulance station was one block from the hospital on the edge of town, but even as they travelled that short distance Phoebe continued to search the streets for the tall, dark fireman. She knew she was being ridiculous. He wouldn't be wandering the streets, he'd be out there, risking his life to save others, but the idea she might never see him again filled her with unexpected despondency.

Steve parked the ambulance and Phoebe stretched as she climbed from her seat. She was filthy, tired and hungry but she knew a shower was pointless as she'd be back out in the heat and smoke soon enough. Dumping her language discs and textbooks on a table, she headed straight for the change rooms. Ripping open the Velcro closures on her fireproof jumpsuit and stripping down to her singlet top, she decided she'd have to be content with a quick wash. Feeling slightly re-freshed, she left the top of her suit dangling from her waist as she walked along the passage back to the kitchen to grab a sandwich. Her stomach rumbled at the thought and she was so focussed on her mission she didn't look where she was going and collided with someone in the passage.

Hands reached out to steady her and she started to apologise, but when she saw who it was the words caught in her throat. Tall, dark and way too attractive.

He was back.

CHAPTER TWO

'SORRY.' Phoebe eventually managed to murmur an apology.

'My fault. Are you OK?' His eyes ran over her body. She knew it was his reaction to the collision but it made her heart race all the same. She cursed her fair skin as she felt a blush steal across her cheeks. She was never normally at a loss for words but she just stood there, staring at him. 'Did I hurt you?'

Phoebe searched for a reply. His hands were still holding her upper arms, making coherent thought difficult. 'No, no.' Her gaze met his and again she felt a sense of familiarity. He held her gaze. Was there a flicker of recognition from him too or was that her over-active imagination?

His lips parted, he was about to speak. She knew she hadn't sounded convincing but she wasn't hurt, only momentarily stunned. 'I'm fine. Really,' she said as she stepped back, forcing him to release her so she could flee to the kitchen where there was safety in numbers. She knew she was being completely absurd, running away from the very person she'd been trying to find all afternoon, but until she could get her ridiculous reaction under control she couldn't be trusted around him. Not if she didn't want him to think her a complete idiot.

She headed for the first familiar face she saw. Ned.

'Hey, Phoebes, how's it going?'

Phoebe deliberately kept her back to the change rooms so she wouldn't be tempted to watch for him.

'Not bad so far, touch wood,' she replied, tapping her knuckles against the tabletop. 'Where've you been today?'

'The other side of Mt Lofty. It's pretty hairy over there.' As an experienced firefighter, if Ned thought a situation was dangerous, Phoebe knew it must be bad. 'I'm heading back in a minute.' He glanced over Phoebe's right shoulder, then reached out to shake someone's hand.

'Max, buddy.' His grin was broad. 'I wasn't expecting you this early.'

The mystery fireman was here. Only he wasn't a mystery to Ned.

Max and Ned merged together in a bear hug. Phoebe saw a flash of blue followed by tanned arms, bulging biceps and dark hair curling at the nape of a strong neck.

The hug over, there were claps on backs and broad grins, illustrating the reunion was a happy one. 'I'm not officially on deck till tomorrow but you know how it is with fires like this. The more the merrier.'

'Phoebe, this is Max. We did our basic training together, he's our relieving station officer, covering for Dutchy. Max, this is Phoebe. We live together.'

Max held out his hand, accompanying the gesture with a broad smile, flashing his perfect teeth again. 'Nice to meet you officially, Phoebe.'

Phoebe took his hand. His grip was firm, his palm smooth and cool to the touch.

'Hello, Max.' His name suited him and she nearly told him so but fortunately came to her senses just in time. He was looking at her so intently again she couldn't hold his gaze. She dropped her eyes and focussed on his chest.

He, too, had stripped down to a singlet but she was willing to bet he looked ten times better in his than she did in hers. Broad shoulders protruded from his top and while his neck wasn't muscle-bound his arms definitely looked as though he spent time lifting weights. She had a weakness for good arms on a man. His singlet top didn't disguise a well-toned abdomen either. There wasn't an unnecessary ounce of weight on him.

She glanced down at her own once-white singlet, which was now an unattractive shade of brown, thanks to the fires. Her breasts, which she was convinced were one cup size too large, were doing their best to escape. She raised her eyes again to discover he was watching her, looking amused, as she stood frowning at her grubby top.

An announcement came over the loudspeaker. 'Attention, attention, 262 and 263 responding to fires west of Lobethal.'

'That's me,' Ned said. 'I'll catch you both later.'

Phoebe went up on tiptoe, kissing Ned's cheek. 'Be careful.'

Max was watching her again. 'Have you eaten?'

he asked. Phoebe shook her head. 'Can I get you a sandwich—ham and cheese?'

She nodded then berated herself as he went to the kitchen. He was upsetting her equilibrium. She never had ham sandwiches. She didn't even like ham. But she accepted it with thanks when he returned, not wanting to give him any more reasons to think she was a complete fool.

Phoebe sat at a table, pushing a pile of books out of the way to make room for her sandwich. Max pulled out a chair, not waiting for an invitation, not thinking he needed one.

'How long have you and Ned lived together?'

'About eighteen months.'

'So it's serious, then?' He and Ned hadn't caught up much in recent times but it surprised him that Phoebe had never been mentioned, even in passing.

Phoebe frowned at him, her fair eyebrows coming together and creating a little crease in her forehead. 'Serious?'

'Living together for that long, it must be, right?'

'Oh. We don't "live together",' Phoebe said, making quotation marks in the air with her fingers. 'We share a house. Separate bedrooms.' She took another bite of the sandwich she seemed not to be enjoying.

'Jumping to conclusions.' But even as he spoke, he knew there was no way the thought of sharing a bedroom with Phoebe hadn't entered Ned's mind. His reputation as a playboy hadn't been without basis and Phoebe certainly wasn't hard on the eye. Tall and blonde, her figure was athletic, with long lean limbs. And she filled out her tank top in all the right places. As if Ned hadn't noticed!

Maybe she and Ned had had a fling—who was to say otherwise? He tried to get his mind off that topic. It wasn't any of his business.

Her voice halted his train of thought. 'You've had a hectic introduction to the town.'

'It was my choice to start early. I like a bit of drama—gets the adrenalin going.'

'Is there enough drama today to keep you satisfied?' She was smiling at him but her smile didn't quite reach her eyes. He could tell she wasn't sure about him, yet he'd swear there had been sparks between them from the moment they'd met. Or was that exactly why she wasn't sure?

'I reckon today just about covers everything.' He eyed the pile of textbooks in front of Phoebe. 'But it looks as though you're expecting a few quiet moments.' He spun the pile of books around, reading the title of the top one. '*French for Beginners.* Are you planning a trip?'

'No. This is my latest craze, learning French. I've got a test tomorrow.'

'*Êtes-vous assez fort en Francais?*'

She looked at him with a bewildered expression. 'I have absolutely no idea what you just said. It was French, right?'

They both laughed then and he said, 'I asked if you were any good.'

Phoebe buried her face in her hands then reappeared with a smile on her face. 'I guess you already know the answer, but I'll see if my vocab stretches so far. *Non.*'

Her smile reached her eyes, she seemed to relax, and Max had to remind himself to act casual and not stare. She'd be attractive no matter what she did, but when her face was graced with a smile—a real, honest-to-goodness laughing-at-herself smile—she was, purely and simply, lovely. Her eyes were pale blue, but in an unusual, not insipid, way and framed by dark eyelashes, which contrasted with her fair eyebrows. When she'd smiled and even now there was a sparkle in them that hadn't been there before and he knew it was egotistical of him, but he liked the idea he'd been the one to add the extra sparkle. Despite the noise and the crowd in the kitchen, they might have been the only two people there. Her smile had totally captivated him.

'I'm obviously a total disaster,' she answered. 'Can you really speak French or are you pulling my leg?'

'I can speak it, though I'm getting rusty. I haven't had much of a chance to exercise my linguistic skills lately.'

She blew some hair off her face and looked downfallen. Adorably so. 'Did you learn French as a child? Apparently it's much easier then, and I'm clinging to the hope that that's why I'm so bad at it, not just that I'm bad, full stop, and too old!'

She didn't look more than twenty-five but he knew better than to comment on a woman's age, especially one who was a relative stranger. 'I spent a few years in Canada.'

'In the French provinces?'

'No. In Saskatchewan. I did an exchange program through the fire department. I dated a French Canadian girl for a while—she taught me.' She'd taught him a few other things, too, about human nature in particular, and he could feel his blood starting to boil at the thought of how foolish he'd been. But it had been a lesson well learned.

'Do you have any tips to pass on?' Phoebe's question brought him back to the present.

'I watched lots of French movies. It's a great way to test comprehension and work on the accent.' He said the words as if in an ad.

Phoebe laughed and her face lit up again. Again, too, he felt that warmth inside that told him he was the one who'd put that light in her eyes. 'A likely excuse. I've always wondered what men see in foreign movies, and an improved accent isn't high on my list of reasons.'

That was a smile he could very quickly get used to. She had little lines at the corners of her eyes—perhaps she was older than she looked—but rather than detract from her looks the lines gave her face more character. 'I can't speak for all men but in my case it was purely educational.'

She held her hands up in mock surrender. 'I'm not doubting you, I'm sure it helped your linguistic skills no end.' She was laughing again. Her laugh was infectious. So much so that he wasn't leaving here until he knew he'd see her again outside work. He wouldn't usually act this quickly—he'd learnt his lesson there—but something about Phoebe was different. Different enough to make him seize the moment, at any rate.

'Are you up for a deal?' She cocked her head to one side, clearly interested. 'If you play tour guide for me, I'll help you with your French.'

'Won't Ned be expecting to be playing host?'

'I know exactly what sights Ned would have on his itinerary: the pubs and clubs and anywhere else he might find the under 25s. I'm assuming you'd know a few other places of local interest.'

'A fair assumption.'

'We have a deal?'

'I'll think about it.' It hadn't been a rebuff, her mannerisms said she was relaxed enough, but he was still a little surprised. He'd expected her to agree, not because he was arrogant but because he was sure she'd reacted to him in the same way he'd reacted to her. There was something there.

Or was he reading the energy between them all wrong? 'I have to get going,' she was saying as she stood, gathering her books. 'I need to make a phone call. Thanks for the sandwich.'

'*Je vous en prie.*'

'Ah…' She stalled, clearly drawing a blank and frustrated with herself for doing so. 'I know that one, truly.' And she clenched her free hand in a fist and shook it at herself. 'All right, I give up.'

'"You're welcome." That's what it means. And it's in the dialogue on page one of your workbook, I saw earlier, so I'd imagine you'll need that for your test.'

She shook her head, gloom falling over her face and making her eyes darker. 'I'm done for.'

Then she rolled her eyes, shook her head and left him to his thoughts.

Perhaps a stint in the country would be more enjoyable than he'd anticipated.

'Attention, attention 261 and 81 responding to an MVA.'

'Sorry, Mum, I have to go, they're paging me.' Phoebe hung up the phone after saying goodbye, relieved to find all was well on her parents' small land holding on the outskirts of town. So far, at least. She raced back to the ambulance bay, shrugging the top of her jumpsuit on as she went.

'What have we got?' she asked Steve, deciding that was quicker than checking her own pager.

'MVA on Jungfer Road. The car's left the road and apparently there's someone trapped inside.'

Phoebe jumped into the driver's seat, waiting until Steve had buckled his seat belt before pulling out of the station, siren blaring. A fire engine was in front of them, leading the way. As they drove further out of town the visibility worsened and Phoebe had to concentrate in order to keep a safe distance between the ambulance and the fire engine while still keeping them within sight. The emergency broadcaster was giving them regular updates on the state of the fires, including where they were burning and in which locations people needed to be making decisions about staying or vacating their properties. Residents of Lobethal were being advised to evacuate now. Jungfer Road was one road that remained open and provided an exit route for those residents. As the ambulance got closer to the turn-off Phoebe drove more cautiously in order to avoid the steady stream of cars coming from the opposite direction. She wanted to put her foot down, she felt the need to get to the crash site as quickly as possible, but she couldn't risk being involved in an accident of her own.

In front of her she saw the flashing left-turn indicator on the fire engine. She flicked her own indicator on, slowing further to take the corner. They drove on for a few minutes but as they approached one of the few bends in the road Phoebe saw a car pulled off to one side. A man climbed out of the car and waved them down. The fire engine pulled over and Phoebe brought the ambulance to a stop behind it.

She jogged past the fire engine, concentrating on getting to the witness to get any information he might have but still vaguely aware of the fire crew already at work, opening hatches and retrieving their equipment. Aware too that Max was among them.

She stopped beside the man's car. 'He's down there.' The elderly man's voice was muffled by the hand towel he was holding over his nose and mouth to protect himself from the hot, ash-strewn air. He pointed with one hand over the embankment and Phoebe looked in the direction he had indicated. She could see an old yellow sedan at the bottom of the slope, its front crumpled around a huge tree.

'I went down there, but I couldn't get any response. Do you think he might be dead?'

They had no way of determining that from where they stood and Phoebe assumed it had been a rhetorical question.

'Did you see the accident?'

'No. My wife and I were travelling behind that car but I lost him as he went around the bend. He was driving pretty fast considering the conditions and I guess he lost sight of the road in the smoke. I thought I'd better wait to show you where the car was—it's not easy to see.'

He was right. The thick smoke was obscuring everything, limiting visibility to less than a hundred metres and, coming from the direction they travelled, they could easily have missed the wrecked car.

'Do you have any idea who's in the car?'

'No. Sorry.' He shook his head. 'Can we get going now, do you think?'

Phoebe could hear a slight tremor in the old

man's voice. He'd done the right thing, what his conscience had demanded of him, and now understandably he was getting nervous about the approaching fire. Phoebe was nervous, too.

'Of course. Thanks for your help.'

He hurried to his car, still clutching the towel to his face.

Phoebe looked around her. Cars continued to travel past but for once they didn't have to work with a crowd of onlookers, the imminent danger from the bushfire was taking care of curious spectators. The fire crew and Steve were already at the vehicle, assessing the situation. Phoebe hurried down the slope, slipping a little on the dry undergrowth with its layer of fallen gum leaves.

The car was a total wreck. The driver's side was wrapped around the tree, the bonnet virtually non-existent now as it was so badly compacted. The windscreen was shattered but access through there was limited as the tree blocked the opening. From what Phoebe could see, it appeared as though the steering-column might have crushed the driver's chest, pinioning him to the wreck. She very much doubted he'd survived the accident.

She saw Max hand the spreaders to Mitch

before coming to her side. Both of them silent, watching, waiting for the firies to get access to the vehicle.

Max spoke first, verbalising her thoughts. 'I don't reckon there'll be much you can do for him even if he is alive.'

There were no signs of movement from within the car and no response to any of their calls. The doors were too badly damaged to be opened so Mitch smashed the back passenger window directly behind the driver, but even that caused no reaction.

As soon as the window was shattered Steve reached through the gap. Phoebe saw him put his hand on the driver's shoulder, heard him ask a question, seeking a response. Nothing.

Steve moved his hand over the driver's neck and Phoebe knew he was checking for a pulse. He cocked his head to one side in concentration.

'I've got a pulse. Weak and irregular but he's still alive. We need access now!'

Max picked up the crowbar Mitch had dropped at his feet and hurried around to the passenger side of the car to smash the unbroken windows while Mitch started cutting through the pillars supporting the roof. It would take Mitch a few minutes to get them access. Minutes this young man might not have.

Phoebe could hear Steve talking to the youth even though there was no response. She felt extraneous and looked for something useful to do. She skirted the tree, the tree that had done all the damage, wondering if there was any way she could get into the car. Was there enough room for her to squeeze through the broken windscreen into the front seat?

No way would she fit. To get through that hole she needed to be about five feet four and weigh eight stone. Not five feet ten and buxom.

Max had smashed the windows on the near side and Phoebe looked at the shattered glass scattered over the seats and littering the floor. A handbag lay on the floor, covered in broken glass, its bright colours incongruous in the wreckage. Phoebe's gaze travelled over the handbag across to Steve. He'd stepped back from the driver, giving Mitch room to cut through the metalwork.

Phoebe's subconscious drew her attention back to the handbag, suddenly working out what was so strange. She stepped back from the car, searching the ground around the crash site.

'What is it?' she heard Max's question.

'There must have been someone else in the car. A girl.'

'What?'

'There's a handbag on the floor. Why would *he* have a handbag? We've got to find her.'

She moved to the front of the car. A flash of bright blue in the undergrowth to her left caught her eye. She wondered how she'd missed it as she'd first skirted the tree.

It was a sandal.

And the sandal was on a foot.

Phoebe's eyes travelled up from the foot, following the line of a jeans-clad leg.

'Over here.'

Max was beside her.

The top half of the body was partially hidden by a straggly shrub and Phoebe stepped forward. It was a girl. She was lying on her stomach but her face was turned towards them, her head at an unnatural angle, her sightless eyes staring into the sky.

'Her neck's broken.'

Phoebe squatted down beside her, force of habit making her check for a pulse even though she knew it was futile. She took her fingers from the girl's neck, reaching up to close her eyelids.

Max looked back to the tree and the destroyed car. 'She must have been flung out on impact.' He stretched out his hand, offering to help Phoebe up. 'Come on, there's nothing you can do for her now.'

Phoebe took his hand. The contact was comforting, his warmth reassuring after touching the lifeless body of the young girl at their feet. In the background Phoebe was aware of the noise of the jaws of life crunching through metal as Mitch cut open the car.

'Are you OK?'

She nodded, an automatic response, but actually she was far from okay. Unnecessary deaths always gave her a mix of emotions. She couldn't remember the last time any of her colleagues had asked if she, or anyone else, was affected by what they dealt with at work. Death was an inevitable part of their job but it didn't mean they were unaffected by it. It never got any easier but no one really talked about it. She didn't need—didn't want—to talk or think about it either. She knew from experience she just needed to keep moving. To stay busy.

Despite the heat of the day she felt a chill as she

moved away from Max's side. Keep moving, stay busy. Max was right. There was nothing she could do for this girl but hopefully they'd be able to save the driver.

The firemen had peeled back the roof of the car along the driver's side and were just removing the front door. Steve was still talking. 'Just about there, mate. Hang on.'

The moment the door was gone Steve was back in place, his hand under the driver's chin, supporting his head, feeling for the carotid pulse. The youth's face was surprisingly undamaged. He had a cut above his eye but that had stopped bleeding and Phoebe knew why even before Steve spoke.

'We've lost him.'

Now the car had been opened up they could see the massive abdominal injuries the lad had suffered. Looking at those, Phoebe was surprised he'd still been alive when they arrived.

Steve let the driver's head go and stood, turning to speak to the policemen who'd just arrived. Max and his crew began gathering their equipment, preparing to return to the fire front. Returning to their task of saving the living.

Phoebe climbed back up the slope with them,

part of her wishing she could leave too. Leave this scene of death and destruction. Leave with Max.

Instead, she dragged a Jordan frame and a sheet from the ambulance and made her way back down the slope, waving a hand in farewell to the firies.

With Steve's help she lifted the girl onto the Jordan frame and covered her with the sheet. Two policemen helped them carry her to the ambulance where they put her on a stretcher and slid her into the van. The police would arrange to collect the car later—the driver would have to be cut out of the wreckage and their resources were already stretched because of the bushfires. Phoebe didn't like leaving the driver behind but with the fire crew gone she didn't have any way to get him out of the car. She had no choice.

She closed the ambulance doors and climbed into the passenger seat beside Steve. Ash was falling around them as they drove away, coating everything with a fine layer of grey, a suitable colour in the circumstances, and how many more fatalities they'd see before the fires were extinguished.

The atmosphere in the ambulance as they left the hospital was subdued. Neither of them liked delivering casualties. Steve was driving so Phoebe picked up the handset of the two-way to notify the station they were back on the road.

'This is Hahndorf 81—we're just leaving the Hahndorf Hospital. Where would you like us to head? Over.'

'Hahndorf 81, please return to the station. The fire has broken containment lines and all non-essential units are being withdrawn from the area. I repeat. Please return to the station. Over.'

Phoebe glanced at Steve. 'Fat lot of good we'll be, sitting at the station,' he said.

'My thoughts exactly, but I don't suppose we have much of a choice.'

'No. But I'd rather be out doing something than sitting around, twiddling our thumbs,' Steve said as he turned into the main street.

'I guess people either get out to us or they don't. They won't risk more lives by sending us into a no-go zone,' Phoebe said, as Steve parked the ambulance and she hopped out. 'I'm just going to the control room. I want to see what the situation is for myself.'

The control room was crowded. It seemed as though many people had had the same idea. If they couldn't be at the scene of the emergency they still wanted to feel involved. Knowing what was going on, even if it was only via a telephone and a fax machine, was preferable to feeling totally useless.

One wall was covered with a large-scale map showing an aerial view of the Hills zone, red markings indicating the area where bushfires were burning. Three separate fires were marked and if the north wind kept up, two of the three fires would be threatening their region, two too many. One fire was already within ten kilometres of Hahndorf, albeit on the other side of the Onkaparinga River.

Phoebe turned to leave the control room. There was nothing she could do there. She saw Steve beckoning to her over the heads of the crowd.

'What's up?' she asked as she met him in the corridor.

'A call's just come through. An eighteen-month-old child with breathing difficulties. His parents are too frightened to move him because of his condition so they called for us.'

'I didn't hear anything over the loudspeaker.'

'We're not being dispatched.'

Phoebe frowned. 'Why not?'

'It's too dangerous.'

'Where's the house?'

'Six k's out of town, this side of the river but in the direct line of the fire.'

'Can we get to them?'

Steve nodded. 'The road's still open but—'

'We've been told to stay put.' Phoebe finished the sentence and Steve nodded. 'What are you thinking?' she asked, although she was pretty sure she knew the answer.

'I'm in. Are you?'

Phoebe wasn't the type of person who regularly broke the rules but this wasn't a rule as such, more a recommendation. She nodded at Steve, both of them already heading to their ambulance, the decision a foregone conclusion.

Minutes later, after being berated over the radio by their team leader for disobeying orders, Phoebe pulled into a dirt driveway lined with tall dark firs. The ambulance's suspension took a beating as they bounced over the potholes in the approach to the red brick cottage. It was a pretty house, surrounded by large lawns and well-tended garden beds that pressed hard up against its walls, but with the dark clouds of smoke rolling in over the bush, like the wolf lurking in the shadows of a story book cottage, the atmosphere was sinister.

Phoebe parked the ambulance in the curve of the driveway. A blast of hot wind caught her in the face as she opened her door. Tiny particles of dust and pollen blew into her eyes, forcing their way behind her sunglasses. She narrowed her eyes as she and Steve grabbed their gear and headed for the porch, the crunch of gravel underfoot barely audible over the roar of the wind. The light was eerie, glowing with the colours of fire, bright in contrast to the backdrop of a dark and ominous sky.

The front door opened and a man stepped out to meet them, shaking their hands in a distracted fashion, looking not at them but at the smoke looming over the bush.

'Malcolm Watts, Benji's dad. He's through here,' he said, beckoning them in and casting a last look in the direction of the fire. It was still out of sight but they all knew it was just over the hill. 'The wind's all over the place, I don't like the look of it.'

Phoebe had to agree and when the front door

slammed shut behind them, closed by the force of the wind, she shuddered at the finality of the sound. Malcolm led the way into a sitting room where a toddler was lying wan and pale on the couch, his blonde head on his mother's lap. The child's skin was almost translucent in the way of infants and young children and his mother was stroking the damp yellow curls back from his forehead. Her focus was entirely on her son. She was oblivious to their arrival.

And it was too much like Joe. This could have been her. That *had* been her, her cheek resting on the velvet roundness of another's little cheek, running fingers through sweet-smelling, soft curls, heart swelling with the impossible sweetness of such a love.

Come snuggle Mumma, Joe. How much do I love you?

Mostly it was OK. Mostly the past didn't rush at her like this, making her breath catch in her throat, her lungs constrict with sudden remembrance. But sometimes…

'Phoebe?'

Steve was already at Benji's side, calling to her, casting a glance to hurry her along.

It wasn't Joe and it wasn't her. She'd had that life, a long time ago. She had a new one now, she was another person to the one she'd been. There was no turning back the clock. Sometimes her memory didn't obey the rules, but she had to. And she always did.

She didn't miss a beat, heading straight over to introduce herself to Benji's mum, Marg, noting at the same time how the little boy's eyes were ringed with dark circles, each exhalation a struggle with a tight wheeze. Steve was already setting up the oxygen cylinder, slipping the mask into place, adjusting the straps until he had the fit right over Benji's nose and mouth. As he moved on to the physical exam, speaking softly to the child, Phoebe questioned Malcolm and Marg about Benji's health history. Benji appeared unfazed by Steve, a stranger, rolling up his top and pressing a stethoscope against his chest. It was a further sign he was a very sick little boy.

'Definite obstruction of the airway, difficulty exhaling.' Steve announced his findings as he continued the examination.

'You say he's been sick these last few days? Wheezing getting worse?' Phoebe asked.

Malcolm nodded and Marg said, 'We didn't take him to the doctor because last month he had the same thing and they said they couldn't do anything—it was just a cold and a slight upper respiratory infection, nothing major. But then this morning he started to wheeze a lot. It's been getting worse. He was crying and now he's settled, but he still can't breathe.'

No point now in explaining he'd not settled but become exhausted. His condition had deteriorated, not improved. 'The wheezing hasn't happened at all before? Your doctor hasn't mentioned asthma?'

'No, nothing like that. We thought he had a cold and we'd stick it out here. We've done it before and it's always been fine. But we didn't have a child then.'

'We should have left. The smoke's made him worse.' Marg's voice cracked with barely restrained feeling as she spoke. 'What's wrong with him? Is it asthma? Is it the smoke?'

'The hospital will have to give you the answers, but it's likely he has undiagnosed asthma. The smoke or the harsh wind whipping up the pollens and dust are all likely triggers.

Wheezing in small children is more likely to be from a cold induced by a virus rather than asthma per se, but Benji's symptoms suggest it's much more than a simple cold.'

Steve was continuing to monitor Benji on the oxygen. 'He's not responding as quickly as I'd hoped.' Phoebe looked at Benji, whose lips were now faintly tinged with blue.

'Nebuliser?'

Steve nodded and Phoebe extracted the nebuliser equipment, setting it up with well-practised hands, running the Ventolin with the oxygen. The ventolin rose, smoke-like, up through the mask and Benji inhaled it, submissive throughout.

'We'll need to take him to hospital.'

'Aren't we meant to stay put?' Marg asked. 'That's why we called the ambulance and didn't leave before.'

'Yes, theoretically, and for the same reason we weren't meant to come out in the first place, but the best place for Benji is the hospital. One of you can ride with us or you can both follow. That is, if you're coming.'

'Of course we're coming,' said Malcolm, adding, 'Do you want to grab some things, Marg?'

He touched her on the arm, the gesture of intimacy and affection jabbing Phoebe in the heart, although she covered it by packing up their equipment. She'd had that, too, that closeness with someone, that sense of being on each other's side.

Or had she? Had it really been like that with Adam before it had all fallen apart?

Malcolm called after his wife, breaking into her thoughts, 'Bring the fire-box, too, just in case, honey.' Marg's eyes widened at that. It seemed that in her anxiety over Benji she'd forgotten for a brief moment about another danger lurking on the horizon.

As Marg collected her thoughts and left the room a new sound intruded.

'Sirens.' Steve and Phoebe spoke in unison.

'It's the CFS siren. The fire must be getting closer,' Malcolm told them. Phoebe shot a look at Steve, wondering if they'd been foolish coming here. But it was too late to worry about that now. They needed a new plan.

'Where's your phone, Malcolm?' Phoebe asked him. 'I'll just let the hospital know we're coming in.'

'The phone lines are down. We just managed to

call 000 before they went and we don't have mobile reception here.'

'I'll use the ambulance two-way, then,' Phoebe said, leaving in what she hoped was an efficient manner, trying to quell the mild panic fluttering about in her belly. 'Back in a moment.'

As she stepped from the house, the first thing she was aware of, after the screaming of the siren, was the hot wind blasting her left side. It had swung around.

Windy days had always unsettled her and coming out into this gale was extremely unnerving. The wind had increased in intensity and buffeted her as she struggled across the driveway. Trees were being bent double by the force of the wind and she made herself keep walking, leaning into the wind, fighting her instinct to return to the safety of the house. She had to find out what the situation was—they couldn't afford to be trapped on the road.

The howling of the wind was battling with the shrieking of the siren, the cacophony of noise clashing in Phoebe's head and making her want to scream in frustration.

She made it to the ambulance, tugging open the door and clambering into the front seat. She picked up the radio but the external noises were so intrusive she knew she wouldn't be able to make herself heard. She put her sunglasses on top of her head and massaged her temples. A flash of light in the rear-view mirror caught her attention. A fire engine was coming up the driveway behind her.

It came to a stop two metres from where she sat.

Four fire officers climbed out and Phoebe knew them all but had eyes for only one.

Max was back.

Which, judging by the immediate pitch in her belly as she took in the broad bulk of him, was a good thing.

Except the three other officers had swung immediately into action, and there was a major fire raging somewhere nearby. So, not so good?

She climbed out of the ambulance and waited as Max issued directions to his men before coming to her, his strides making short work of the distance, his gait giving no indication of the heaviness of the protective clothing all the firemen wore. He wore his helmet but had his visor up and over one shoulder he'd slung an oxygen cylinder. He looked like a man in control.

'Max! What's going on?' Over Max's shoulder Phoebe could see his crew working in an efficient but hurried manner. Two were unrolling hoses while the third was taking more oxygen cylinders from the truck.

Max answered her question with one of his own. 'What are you doing here?'

'There's a little boy inside, suffering a serious asthma attack. We're just about to take him out to the hospital.'

'Not right now you're not. You need to get back inside.' Phoebe felt Max's hand in the small of her back as he tried to guide her in the direction of the house.

'I need to get Benji to hospital.'

'Phoebe, I don't have time to argue. You need to listen to me.'

A trickle of sweat snaked its way down her spine. 'What's happening?'

'This wind change has whipped the fire back on itself and it's heading straight for us.' Max took a few seconds before he answered. 'The road's been cut off. You're not going anywhere.'

CHAPTER THREE

'PLEASE, tell me you're kidding.'

'I wish I was. Go inside.' He pinned her with a look that said this was non-negotiable. 'I'll be there shortly.'

'What are you going to do?'

'Our job.'

Phoebe saw Max nod towards his men and suddenly realised he didn't have time to convince her—she had to do as he asked. She nodded, spun around and headed for the house.

Once she was gone Max turned his attention back to his crew, relieved to find they were well prepared.

'Cookie, you and Mitch get started on wetting down the house, check the gutters and get any roof sprinklers going. Nifty and I'll take the BA gear inside and check out the situation there, then we'll be back to give you a hand.'

Cookie and Mitch nodded and Max left them to it. He grabbed his helmet from the front seat before picking up a couple of cylinders and the breathing apparatus face masks and racing indoors.

Inside was a complication he hadn't anticipated until he'd seen Phoebe and the ambulance.

Civilians.

His crew had been using the property's dam water to refill the fire engine's water tank when they'd been alerted that the fire had swung round. Their only option had been to retreat to the house but Max hadn't expected to find it occupied. His first responsibility was to his crew and their safety but his second responsibility was to try to ensure there were no fatalities. He wasn't sure how he was going to manage that but he was determined to do his best. He now had eight other people depending on him.

He left Nifty with Malcolm, knowing he could trust him to sort out the practicalities of things like ladders and sprinklers while he did a quick check of the house, looking for the safest place, knowing there was going to come a time, probably sooner rather than later, when they'd all need to go to ground and hopefully sit out the fire.

What he didn't know was how successfully they'd be able to do that.

He finished his inspection and made his way into the lounge where Malcolm, his family, Phoebe and Steve waited. Waited for direction from him.

Phoebe was the first to speak. 'What can we do?'

Max thought it was highly unlikely that anything they did inside the house would improve their odds but telling them that would be counter-productive. He needed everyone to stay calm, or as calm as possible, and in all probability that meant keeping them occupied.

His gaze went to the little boy lying on the couch. 'How's Benji doing?'

'His oxygen sats are improving. He's stabilising.'

That was some good news. If his condition wasn't deteriorating, that would help to keep everyone else calmer.

'All right. We're already starting to see spot fires from embers blown ahead of the fire front. That's the biggest danger to the house at the moment. Embers can get blown through small cracks so you need to soak towels and block up any gaps under doors and windows. Windows can crack and break with the temperature changes so all the curtains need to come down and furniture needs to be moved away from windows to reduce the chance of flammable materials igniting if embers do come in. You'll need to keep checking the house, watching out for any gaps or embers. Grab as many dry woollen blankets as you can find and pile them by the cellar stairs. There's a ladder under the manhole but one of us will check the ceiling cavity for embers.' He looked around the group, noting their attention was firmly fixed on him. 'OK, is that clear?'

'Close doors and windows, take down curtains, wet towels into gaps, blankets. Got it.' Phoebe repeated his instructions.

No one seemed to be panicking—that, at least, was a good sign. 'Right. I'll leave you guys to it but we'll be back inside before long.' He tried to convey a confidence he was having trouble feeling. In his opinion the odds weren't in their favour but luckily no one asked him that. Did they all assume they'd be OK or didn't they want to ask because they were scared of what they might hear?

Max left them to it and Phoebe's confidence followed him out the door. She had to force herself to concentrate and remember the tasks he'd allocated. Doors, windows, curtains. What had he said about the ceiling? She looked up. She'd never have considered checking the roof space, and wondered what other direction danger would come from.

'Steve, why don't you keep an eye on Benji, seeing as you've been monitoring him? I'll do the patrol,' Phoebe said. She knew she was asking partly for selfish reasons. She wanted to feel as if she had some control over events and was making some sort of contribution towards keeping everyone safe. 'Malcolm, can you show me where the towels and blankets are? Then we can sort out the house.'

Malcolm quickly directed Phoebe to the linen closet, bathroom and laundry and they divided the house into two and started wetting towels and shoving them under the external doors and windows. Phoebe then filled up as many buckets and other assorted containers as she could find with water and left them at strategic points in each room, ready to extinguish any embers should it be necessary.

Malcolm was filling the last few buckets so

Phoebe started taking down curtains. As she moved around the house, she was able to catch of a glimpse of the fire crew. Despite the fact they were all covered from head to toe, including flash hoods and goggles over their faces, topped by helmets, she knew when it was Max, the sheer size of him giving him away even before she saw his easy gait and powerful stride. He was still extinguishing spot fires with the hand-held water sprayer. Surely he couldn't continue doing that for much longer as, much as she hated to admit it, even she could see he was fighting a losing battle.

She finally got all the curtains down and did another check of the doors but the waiting was awful. The fire was coming—coming straight for them unless, by some miracle, the wind changed again—and she found herself wishing it would hurry up and arrive. Or at least that something would happen to distract her from this feeling of waiting for the inevitable and being the only one with nothing productive to do about it.

As she stood there, wishing for something to happen, the lights went out. In the sudden darkness she could see the glow of the fire more clearly. The only source of light was coming from the brightly burning bush and in the sudden darkness, and accentuated by the silence, the wind sounded more ferocious and Phoebe started to feel more than slightly nervous.

Embers were flying through the air now, igniting spot fires all around the house as they landed. She watched as a spot fire burnt brightly a few metres from the house. Max appeared, dousing the fire, extinguishing it as quickly as it had started. He saw her in the window and gave her a thumbs-up before striding out of sight, leaving her alone to her strange, solitary watch.

She grabbed a torch and paced through the house, moving from room to room, checking on Steve and Benji, double-checking the wet towels and topping up water basins. The sky was black now and she could see flames jumping from treetop to treetop on the next ridge, could hear the dreadful sound of the fire roaring like a wild animal as it devoured everything in its path. It was close now, too close, and still Max was outside.

Phoebe stopped pacing in the kitchen. The windows here faced east and looking out she could see a towering wall of fire racing across the land. The spot fires were inconsequential now in the face of the ferocity of the main blaze. She scanned the garden for Max as she stood at the sink, filling bottles of water, but could see no one. Where had they gone?

Watching the fire approach, Phoebe couldn't believe they were safe in the house. Surely the fire would destroy everything in its path? It was far too late to make a run for it. The wall of flame was greedily seeking out any fuel—undergrowth, trees and hay bales alike were being consumed.

She jumped as the outside door opened and four firefighters swarmed inside. They were all carrying oxygen cylinders and breathing apparatus. Three didn't stop, just headed through the kitchen before peeling off in different directions, two to the front of the house and one to the ladder in the manhole. The fourth put down his load before removing his goggles and flash hood. Max. His hair was curling and damp with sweat. He wiped one forearm across his brow, leaving a dark streak of soot and sweat on his skin.

Phoebe passed him a water bottle and he took a long drink as she went to the back door to shove the wet towel back into the gap. She caught Max's expression as she stood up. He obviously thought she was wasting her time.

'That's not going to help, is it?'

'No.' Max shook his head and for the first time since the bushfire had started Phoebe was truly afraid.

'How long have we got?'

'Ten minutes, maybe more, maybe less.'

'What do we do now?'

'Get everyone down into the cellar and stay there.'

'Are we going to be OK?'

Her pale blue eyes were enormous, their unusual colour accentuated against the dust coating her nose and cheeks. Max checked his impulse to wipe the soot from her face. Forcing himself to concentrate on the job at hand, a dangerous job that really needed his undivided attention, he replied to her question.

'I honestly don't know.' As he answered he saw Cookie reappearing from the manhole. Cookie gave him a thumbs up before making his way to the cellar steps in the passage outside the kitchen. Max counted heads as people retreated to the relative safety of the cellar. He knew there were no guarantees they'd get through this. If the house became engulfed by the bushfire, their chances were pretty low, but the cellar was their best option.

Seven people, carrying an assortment of blankets, oxygen cylinders, torches and water bottles, disappeared from view.

'Time to go.' He picked up the last two cylinders and nodded towards a torch and a water bottle sitting on the table. 'Might as well grab those, too.' He had a quick glance at his watch—4.05 p.m.—before checking the room one last time. He didn't expect to be in the cellar for long. The fire was moving so fast it wouldn't take long to pass by. The only question was, would they still be here after it had roared through?

He ushered Phoebe in front of him towards the cellar. As they reached the doorway a loud explosion occurred, startling them both. Phoebe jumped, the beam of her torch lighting up the passage ceiling, and Max collided with her.

'What was that?' She turned to face him, a look of terror on her face.

'Gum trees, I expect. They heat up in the fire and they explode.' Max didn't tell her that quite often that would be how the fire spread.

Another explosion got Phoebe moving again and Max followed her down the stairs.

The cellar wasn't huge and the floor space they had at their disposal wasn't much bigger than a hospital lift. The others were already sitting on the floor in a semi-circle, Mitch, Steve, Cookie, Malcolm, Marg and Nifty. Benji was lying in Marg's lap, opposite Steve.

Despite the fact the cellar was several degrees cooler than the rest of the house, it was still hot. Max knew his thick fireproof clothing didn't help matters but he was reluctant to remove his jacket, its protective qualities were too important. His crew were all still wearing their full kits, too, and the others had thick woollen blankets over their shoulders. Everyone would be feeling the heat.

Max wrapped a spare blanket around Phoebe, taking care to leave a decent portion of it around her shoulders. 'Pull this over your head if I tell you to.'

She nodded, and he could sense the nervous tension running through her. Her shoulders were tense, her back rigid, but, like all of them, she was maintaining a calm façade.

He put his oxygen cylinder on the floor and sat in the only free space at the base of the stairs, pulling Phoebe down with him. Each member of his crew would need to share their tank with a civilian—the reason Mitch, Cookie and Nifty had positioned themselves where they were.

Max checked his watch again—4.10 p.m. the fire front must be almost on them. It was becoming more difficult to breathe as the fire sucked all the oxygen from the air. They needed to conserve their energy and that meant keeping their chatter to a minimum. He held up the auxiliary mouthpieces and spoke to the people huddled around him.

'We'll share our oxygen with you—you'll need to breathe through these mouthpieces. Just breathe normally through your mouth, regular breaths.'

Max settled Phoebe between his knees, her back tucked against his front. The auxiliary line was short and the lack of space meant they couldn't sit face to face and for that Max was grateful as he knew he'd find that too distracting. He opened the valve on his cylinder, pulled his mask over his face and then handed the auxiliary mouthpiece to Phoebe.

He checked the room—from what he could see in the torchlight, everyone appeared to be breath-

ing comfortably. They might not need supple-
mentary oxygen but Max figured the unusual
activity gave everyone something else to concentrate on and would hopefully serve to keep their
minds off the bushfire.

Phoebe shifted her position slightly, the
movement momentarily pushing her bottom
further into Max's lap, before she settled into a
more comfortable spot. One that didn't leave her
pressed into his groin. The cellar might just be
large enough to accommodate four firefighters,
four adult civilians and one child but it wasn't big
enough for him to escape his growing awareness
of one very womanly woman.

He was caught between a rock and a hard place,
although he wasn't complaining. Since this was
the situation they were in, at least he was the one
who had the opportunity to reassure Phoebe.
Then again, maybe it was a cruel joke. They were
in a situation he was all too aware could spell
death for all involved, he was holding a woman
he was seriously attracted to, and they were stuck
in a cellar with a mob of other people, meaning
there wasn't a damn thing he could do about
acting on his attraction. He looked around for a

distraction, anything to get his mind off the round firmness of Phoebe's backside as she shifted again to tuck the blanket underneath her.

But there were no other distractions. There was nothing to do but sit and wait. The breathing apparatus made conversation impossible so there was literally nothing left to do except sit and think.

He checked his watch for the third time—4.20 p.m. Fifteen minutes had passed. He'd give the fire another five minutes before checking the situation. By then they'd either be safe or—He didn't want to think about the alternative.

Phoebe's blonde hair was shining in the dim light, reflecting the meagre light of the torches. She looked golden and perfect, epitomising everything that was good in the world, and he promised himself then and there that if they survived the day, he'd ask her out.

To dinner, to lunch, to loitering in the grocery aisle. Frankly, he didn't care where they went or what they did. Just as long as she said yes. He couldn't ignore the feeling of having something fantastic dangled in front of him and not being able to act on it. He couldn't ignore the frustration that was almost as bad as having to sit out a fire front in a cellar, not knowing if they'd make it through. And he preferred thinking about that frustration rather than the likely outcome of the fire front ripping through the house.

So that was one miracle for the day, the fact he was thinking about asking a woman out. He hadn't for so long, he couldn't remember the last time. No, that was a lie. He knew exactly who he'd last been with, who had shattered his trust so he'd avoided any involvement since. Which begged the enormous question of what it was about Phoebe that had so got under his skin. The intensity of their current predicament?

No firefighter would ever choose to be where they were right now, with the odds stacked so heavily against them and nothing more to be done to increase the chance of survival. Men weren't made to sit and wait, they were made to act. To face extreme danger with no ability to take action was much, much worse than facing it head on and *doing* something. And if that was true for men in general, it was doubly so for firemen.

It sounded reasonable that the enormity of the danger they were in had created this hyper-aware-ness of Phoebe, because then this crazy, unexpected attraction would fade away if—when—they made it out of here. But his awareness of her, this undeniable tightening in his gut, had started almost the moment he'd first seen her. There was something about her, beyond what she looked like—good-looking women weren't a rarity in his life, but recently he'd felt a lack of interest. Yet here was this woman, now nestled between his thighs, her back pressed against his fireproof jacket, the fabric of which was so thick that by rights he shouldn't be aware of the feel of her at all.

But he was.

She was strong and brave and warm and vulnerable all at once. And he'd never met anyone like her.

And since he couldn't do anything more to increase the odds of them all walking out of here alive, it was impossible to stop his mind from focussing on the soft brush of her hair as she leant back a little further and a strand of it fell against his cheek. It was impossible not to wish he could turn her to him and find her mouth with his with a kiss that was raw and hungry and urgent.

But he couldn't do any of that, not when he had a cellar full of people under his care as they waited for a wall of hungry flames to roar over their heads. Maybe if he had been a junior firefighter he would've risked it—and taken his chances of being disciplined if they made it out of here. But he was in charge, so it wasn't an option.

He just had to hope like hell for two miracles—one, that Phoebe would turn out to be as fascinating as she seemed and, two, that they'd make it out alive.

The wind increased in intensity as they waited, howling around the house, rattling windows and shaking walls. The roof timbers creaked and groaned under the force of the wind and in the background was the roar of the fire. The flames would be leaping from treetop to treetop, threatening to devour the house. And them along with it.

If the fire took hold in the roof, they didn't stand a chance.

Phoebe half turned towards him and buried her face in his shoulder. He knew she was unaware of her actions. Involuntarily he wrapped her in his arms, silently offering comfort. She felt good nestled against him, head tucked to one side. She was a perfect fit.

Max looked around the circle. Malcolm had one arm around his wife, offering physical comfort, while Marg was cradling Benji as if a mother's love could protect him from the menacing force of mother nature.

Suddenly the house gave an almighty shudder and then lay silent. As quickly as the wind had picked up, it abated. Had the impossible happened? Had the house escaped? Had they escaped?

The sudden silence brought everyone out of their reveries. Phoebe shifted her weight. Max wasn't sure whether she was conscious of his arms around her but he let them drop, suddenly feeling conspicuous in the close confines of the cellar.

He lifted himself backwards and sat on the bottom step before pushing himself upright. He pulled his mask off and spoke to the group. 'I'm going up. I won't be more than ten minutes.' All three members of his fire crew checked and adjusted their watches, marking the time. His oxygen was nearly depleted so he disconnected his mask, reattaching it to a spare cylinder that had been placed to the side of the stairs. 'Phoebe,

Mitch will share his oxygen with you if necessary.' There were no spare face masks so Phoebe would have to share with Mitch and Steve. Max couldn't afford to go upstairs without his BA. He pulled his mask back into position and slung the full cylinder over his shoulder.

'I'll come. It'll be quicker with two of us checking.' Nifty stood up and Max passed him a second cylinder.

They climbed the stairs, Max leading but not hurrying. He needed to conserve his energy and his oxygen. His cylinder might only last ten minutes if his breathing was too rapid.

'I'll check the roof space,' Nifty said as they emerged from the cellar into the almost comparable gloom of the house. He headed for the manhole as Max went straight to the eastern side of the house, desperate to see for himself where the fire had got to.

It was moving away from the house, heading east, unbelievably leaving the house unscathed. Had wetting the house down saved it from burning or had Malcolm's fire break around the perimeter given them enough of a buffer? Max suspected that they'd just been lucky and had been saved by a last-minute wind change. Whatever the reason, the crisis had been averted and they'd lived to tell the tale.

He dumped his breathing apparatus in the kitchen and picked up one of the water sprayers as Nifty reappeared.

'All clear in the roof.' Nifty glanced out the kitchen window, watching the fire retreat. 'We were bloody lucky.'

'No argument there,' Max said as he pulled his goggles and gloves out of his jacket pocket, sliding his left glove on to turn the doorhandle, mindful it could be holding a lot of latent heat, and stepped outside. Nifty followed and they headed to opposite sides of the back door to circle the house, checking for any spot fires. Max put out a couple of small fires that were burning half-heartedly while he made a quick check of the gutters and roof line. He met Nifty at the front of the house, relieved to see the fire engine and ambulance had also come through the fire unscathed.

He opened the passenger door of the fire truck, using his gloved left hand, and picked up the radio to check in with the station. They'd be waiting for some communication from him.

As soon as he got the all-clear he gave a thumbs-up to Nifty, who hustled back inside to inform the others. By the time Max returned to the house the group of survivors was upstairs and eager to get out. They were drawn to the windows, wanting to confirm that the danger really had passed.

'The road's open—you can take Benji through to town now,' Max told Phoebe and Steve.

'How's our truck, mate?' Steve asked. 'Our heads will be on the chopping block if that's gone up in smoke.'

'No worries. The fire didn't touch it.'

'I think we might still have a bit of explaining to do. We disobeyed instructions,' Phoebe commented.

'We'll be all right. Luckily there was no harm done.' Steve picked up the oxygen cylinder and nebuliser which he'd taken off Benji. 'Let's get on our way.' Marg grabbed the bag she'd packed earlier and which was still lying in the lounge and Malcolm carried Benji out to the ambulance.

Max went with them, opening doors and checking things weren't too hot. Steve, Marg and Benji climbed in the back, Malcolm sat in front with Phoebe. Max waited until Phoebe had buckled herself in before starting to close the door.

Phoebe put one hand out, holding the door open. 'Will you be following us in to town?'

Max shook his head. 'We're heading back to the fire. Our day won't be over for a long while yet.'

Phoebe looked at him closely. 'Be careful.' She touched him on the sleeve, tentatively, and the look on her face suggested there was more she wanted to say. Nifty walked within hearing distance and, having glanced his way, she seemed to change her mind and all she said was, 'And thank you.'

He dipped his head, acknowledging her thanks, and closed the door for her, watching as the ambulance drove away. What would she have done if he'd kissed her just now? Which was what he'd been tempted to do, sorely tempted, until Nifty had come on the scene and changed the mood.

He didn't know what she'd have done, but he did know he'd be seeing her again.

Thoughts of his reaction when he'd held her in the cellar swirled through his mind, as did his resolve at that time. Dinner, lunch or the grocery aisle, he knew it didn't matter. He'd be seeing her again.

Soon. He'd make sure of it.

CHAPTER FOUR

IT WAS the humming that woke him from a fitful night of dreaming.

Dreams not of the fire—his work life never troubled his sleep—but of Phoebe. Phoebe reciting French verbs in the most woeful accent, Phoebe standing on a chair inside the house yesterday as she struggled to bring down a heavy pair of curtains, Phoebe's eyes wide searching for reassurance as the full gravity of the fire front dawned on her. Phoebe feeling so very, very right wrapped in his arms.

So she was here, or rather he was here, in her home, which was not what he'd have predicted this time yesterday when they'd first met. Disentangling himself from the sleeping bag Ned had tossed him in the early hours of the morning when they'd stumbled in from the fires, he pulled on an old pair of tracksuit bottoms and followed the sound of Phoebe humming and the rich aroma of coffee to the kitchen.

Phoebe was reaching for a mug on the top shelf, her T-shirt leaving a strip of skin, shiny with sweat, exposed above barely-there running shorts. Her hair was scrunched without ceremony into a rubber band, her feet bare but with the little imprints of sock elastic around her ankles. She'd been exercising already? Phoebe and coffee was a start to the day he could get used to.

She turned, mug in hand, and jumped when she saw him. 'Max? What are you—?'

'I take it Ned didn't leave you a note?'

She shook her head, tugging the bottom of her T-shirt down. Was she uncomfortable with how she looked in running shorts—without reason—or was she uncomfortable with him being there?

'Is the fire under control?' She'd stopped fiddling with her top, all her attention now focussed on him and news of the fire. That was another thing he could get used to: Phoebe's attention all to himself.

'Finally. The wind blew through, the temperature dropped and we might even get some rain later today.'

'And you? Here?'

'No room at the inn.' He shrugged, his gesture an apology, too. 'By the time I knocked off and got to the pub it was overflowing with local families who've lost their homes or at least been evacuated, so there they were and—'

'And here you are…' She let her sentence trail off, and there was no way of knowing if she minded or not. Except she was shaking her head and chewing on her bottom lip, arms crossed over her chest.

'The station's overrun with the extra night shift,' he added by way of the additional explanation she seemed to need. So she acted as laid-back as the blokes at the station, but perhaps it *was* an act. 'Ned thought it'd be fine, and I admit I'd had it so I didn't push the issue. I'm sorry if—'

'No.' She stopped him with a smile and appeared to gather herself. 'Don't be sorry, it's no problem at all. Of course it isn't.' Which of them was she trying to convince? It was too late now, either way, because he was there, in her kitchen. He was all too aware of her in her skimpy outfit, all too aware that a little over twelve hours ago she'd been sitting in a cellar, wrapped in his arms.

Did she know he'd been about to kiss her yesterday? Was that the source of her uncertainty?

That was too many questions for a sleep-deprived man with no caffeine on board.

'Coffee?'

He sighed, and her face lit up as she laughed at him. 'I take it that's a yes?'

'That'd be great.' So just like that she was OK with him being there? She must have done some fast adjusting because she'd looked like a startled rabbit when he'd walked in on her.

'Make yourself at home. Have a seat,' she said as she nodded to a row of mismatched stools under the high kitchen table. She turned her back to pour the coffee and Max involuntarily let his gaze drop. The view from behind was every bit as good as the view from the front, so he closed his eyes and forced himself to think about what she was saying, not what she was wearing. Or wasn't wearing.

Phoebe turned her head. 'Sugar?'

'Two,' he answered. She looked surprised. Was it because he'd been sitting there with his eyes shut or was it because he wanted sugar? 'Heaped spoons,' he added.

Her eyebrows rose even further. 'You'll be telling me you're a farm labourer or a trades-man next—isn't that their standard coffee order?'

'I didn't know there was such a science to it,' he said, teasing her. 'What about you? Skinny decaf with milk from goats fed on the summer grasses of a western-facing meadow?'

She didn't miss a beat. 'Eastern. And spring. The summer grasses are much too bitter.'

She poured bubbling milk from a saucepan into two cups, topping them up with rich coffee from the espresso pot on the stove. 'I suppose you want marshmallows, too.'

'If you have them, sure.'

'Unbelievably, we do.' She had her back to him again while she fossicked for marshmallows in the pantry. The girl had legs. There was no way Ned could be living with her and not have made a move. He'd corner him and find out, see what Ned's intentions were before he asked her out. She sauntered over and slid the jar across the counter to him. 'Winter nights are cold here. Ned and I are partial to a mug of hot chocolate snuggled under a blanket while we watch TV.'

'Snuggled under a blanket together? Cosy.'

'Two mugs, two blankets. Comfortable, not cosy.'

'What's not cosy?' Ned appeared, wearing nothing but a towel wrapped around his waist. Phoebe didn't blink so it must be his usual morning style. Yet they maintained there was nothing to tell?

'You and me. Max still doesn't believe we haven't got together. Ever. Even one night under the blanket with marshmallows.'

His expression mock mournful, Ned shook his head. 'Believe me, I've begged, but she's pretty mean when it comes to sharing marshmallows. Although,' he said, mug in hand, 'I see she's slipped you the whole jar.'

'Ned! You told me football training is about to start and you need to watch your diet. You asked for my help!'

Ned held both hands up in mock surrender. 'I know, I know. I have no willpower.'

'*And* I thought you were trying to cut down on your sugar intake.'

Ned froze, his sugar-laden spoon poised over his mug. Treating them to a dramatic sigh, he moved the spoon back to the sugar pot before his resolve weakened and he tipped the entire spoonful into his drink.

'Max.' Her expression was baleful but her eyes were full of mirth. 'I'm fighting a one-woman battle.'

'Sorry.' He shrugged. 'I have to agree with Ned. Two sugars is the only way to drink coffee.'

'Why don't men have any willpower? Ned doesn't know the meaning of the word "enough".'

'You wouldn't be referring to my social life would you, Phoebes?'

'I know your thoughts in that regard, Ned Kellaway. So many women, so little time—that's your motto isn't it?'

Max drained the last of his coffee. 'Glad to see you haven't changed, Ned.'

'Mate, I'm nothing if not consistent.' He shot Phoebe a look. 'Don't say anything, we can't all be celibate.'

Celibate? This was an interesting start to the day.

'And we don't all refuse to change out of our work gear before we go to the pub so we can advertise to the ladies how hot we are.' Her voice was teasing, but from the tinge of red that crept up around Ned's neck, she'd been speaking the truth.

'Using the uniform for ulterior gain?' Max drawled. 'Shame on you.'

'Push off, the lot of you,' said Ned. 'I'm just married to my job, man, that's all,' He laughed. 'Whereas you,' he said to Max, 'are apparently still wedded to that band of yours, and you...' he pointed at Phoebe, who raised her eyebrows to the heavens '...are apparently married to your continuing adult education courses.' Phoebe made a show of peeling a banana and paying him no attention but Max's interest was piqued—she'd tensed when Ned had said 'married' to her. Why? What was going on? And what did any of it have to do with being celibate?

And Ned's face when he'd said 'married' had said even more: he'd frozen for a split second like he'd said something unforgivable, then started fussing about with his coffee-cup at the sink. Why?

Her mouth full of banana, Phoebe didn't reply so he got no further clues. He was sure that was her idea, to end the conversation before it went somewhere she didn't want it to. How did he know that? He wasn't sure, but there'd been so many undercurrents zinging around in the last minute he'd have to be unconscious not to be aware of them.

Ned cleared his throat. 'I'd better get dressed and I'll grab you a towel for the shower Max. What are your plans today, Phoebes?' Was that an experienced change of subject he'd just witnessed?

'Steve and I have to make a formal report about why we took the ambulance out yesterday.' She rolled her eyes.

'Are you in strife?'

'We had the informal "please explain" yesterday. I think we'll be OK. I'm hoping it's just a matter of procedure rather than anything too dreadful.'

'And tonight? Are you going to meet us at the pub for karaoke after your French class?'

'Us? Who's in tonight?'

'The usual motley crew should be there for a laugh. Max is coming too—claims he's up for his introduction to the night life of Hahndorf.'

She swallowed the last mouthful of banana and tossed the skin into the compost bin. 'Is that what you call it?' She turned to Max. 'Are you sure you want to have your eardrums mangled by wannabes belting out their version of hits? And is watching Ned strutting around in his uniform, serenading girls barely out of their teens, your idea of entertainment?'

His eyes filled with appreciation at the picture she painted. 'Sounds too good to miss. I might have to get up on the stage myself.' Phoebe threw him a horrified look and he hoped she was joking that the idea of him on stage was so appalling.

'It's amateur night, mate, no guitars allowed,' Ned said.

'You play the guitar?' Phoebe asked. 'Are you any good?'

'He's good enough to have an unfair advantage if he brings it tonight,' Ned answered. 'He's in a band.'

'I promise I'll leave it behind. Along with my firefighting uniform.' He paused for emphasis. 'I don't need to rely on props.' He fixed Ned with a look. 'Like some.'

Phoebe swallowed. Hard, because Max was right. He wouldn't need any props, he had plenty of killer charm all on his own, which made it essential for her to find something to distract herself with. Now, right this second. The coffeepot was as good as anything. He must think she and Ned were more than strange, rinsing out dishes every few minutes, but she had to do *something*. And she hadn't even wanted the first banana, so that ruled out a second. What was Ned thinking, bringing Max home?

And did Max know he had charm to spare? Sitting there all bare-chested and tousled and deliciously rumpled from sleep? He had to know it. Sure of himself, comfortable in his skin, built like—well, like a fireman—and gorgeous-looking to boot. He had to know it. Which would normally have her running in the opposite direction—you couldn't be friends with men who were gorgeous and knew it, they were always so busy thinking about how *you* must be thinking they were wonderful.

And being friends with men was now her specialty. Romance, no. And being friends with women? No, no, triple no. At her age, it invariably led to discussions of marriage and children. And those were topics she steered clear of, she reminded herself as she grabbed a tea-towel and started to dry the coffeepot with great gusto. But getting back to Max, he didn't look like friend material. Her body was giving her strong hints that *it* didn't see him in that light, at any rate. But it seemed as though he was missing the final ingredient that would usually be enough to write off someone who looked like him, even from her list of potential friends: arrogance. Or rather absolute conviction that he was God's gift to the world in general and women in particular.

'What are you saying?'

He was laughing at her.

'What?'

'Your lips are moving while you reassemble—with great care, I might add—that coffee-pot.' There was a smile on his face that almost had her swooning. This was seriously inconvenient. She didn't do attraction.

'Anything in particular you're reciting? French verbs?'

Tell him the truth? As if! 'Yes,' she lied.

'Which one?' The twinkle in his eye said he didn't believe her for a second.

She opened her mouth to lie again and found she couldn't remember a single French verb, let alone how to conjugate one.

'Stage fright? Isn't the big test tonight?'

Too late she forgot she was trying to lie and nodded.

'Well, then, I shall get out of your hair and leave you to study.'

And just like that the men left the kitchen and Phoebe was alone. She'd have to wait for the shower so she may as well run through a few more verbs. She made her way to her favourite spot in the old house, the window-seat in the small library. Her textbooks were on the cushion and she curled up in the corner and looked out over the valley. The glorious view was looking a little hazy today. The smoke from the bushfires continued to hang over the blackened hills to the north but the bush immediately in front of her was unspoiled.

She picked up a textbook, flicking through the pages, but she couldn't concentrate. Images of Max kept popping into her head. How capable he'd been during yesterday's drama, how safe she'd felt in his presence. How good he'd looked this morning without his shirt on and how wonderful she'd felt yesterday wrapped in his arms.

Her gaze drifted out to the gardens again, landing on her favourite outdoor spot on the property, the waterhole nicknamed the Shady Pool. The temperature today wasn't nearly as unpleasant as yesterday but it was still already in the low thirties. Knowing she wasn't going to get any productive revision done, she put her book down, deciding instead to have a swim before her shower. That activity would have the added bonus of getting her out of the house when Max and Ned headed off to work so she wouldn't need to see Max until that night. Maybe by that time she would have had a chance to sort out her thoughts.

Then the feeling of being held by him flooded warmly through her again and she knew sorting out her thoughts before tonight was a long shot.

That was without even thinking about that one moment before Nifty had appeared beside the ambulance. That one moment when she'd thought Max had been about to kiss her.

Had he been? And what would she have done if he had?

It didn't take a lot of thinking—any thinking!—to know exactly what she would have done.

She would have kissed him right back. Then crossed her fingers and hoped for more.

She'd managed to avoid Max all day but had pretty quickly given up hope of escaping her random thoughts of being kissed by him. So she was not surprised when, the moment she pushed open the heavy front door of the pub, it was Max she automatically looked for.

Would he be here?

He was.

All six feet two of him, slouched with grace against the bar, chatting to the barmaid as she poured him a beer.

She hesitated. If it had been Ned, or Steve, or any other of the men she worked and socialised with, she wouldn't think twice, she'd be up there with them, ordering a drink, teasing, chatting. Acting like a normal person instead of a starstruck adolescent. But it wasn't any of those safe men. It was Max. Which meant…

She wasn't sure yet what it meant. Undecided, she stood near the door and watched, feeling like the new kid at school. How was that fair? She'd lived here far longer than Max yet he had an enviable ease in his surroundings. The way he sat, moved, talked—he seemed without selfconsciousness, at ease in his skin. Had she ever felt like that? She wasn't sure, but she knew nowadays she never really felt easy anywhere. The past was always lurking just out of sight, reminding her not to get too comfortable. There was no point in letting down your guard only to have disaster tap you on the shoulder again.

'Phoebe.' He'd spotted her dithering about by

the door and was waving her over, his face alive with good health.

A deep breath got her legs moving and she wove her way between the people standing between them.

Holding out an arm, he drew her in for a kiss on the cheek as if it were the most natural thing in the world, asking her at the same time what he could get her to drink and turning back to the waitress without missing a beat. Whereas she was still trying to get her racing heart to settle down. One touch on the cheek, one feather-light brush from his lips and she was on fire.

'How was the test?'

A simple enough question, so why did it make her feel he had her well-being so much at heart? She'd refused to let herself enjoy a man's attentions for too long, that was all, and this one had sneaked in before she could run a mile or get her defences up.

'I passed.' He had her drink, and led her through to the next room, over to the usual booth she shared with Ned, saved for them by Ned's huge fire-jacket dumped on the tabletop. They slid in, looking about the room as they shrugged out of their jackets. 'At least, I think I passed. Tonight was just the written exam—we have an oral next week.'

She was screwing up her deliciously shaped nose. 'And it's the oral I'm worried about.'

He threw back his head and laughed. 'This is a casual language course, right? You're not going to the guillotine if you don't pass.'

She shrugged, pushing out her bottom lip in such a way that he wanted to pull her into his arms and kiss away her anxieties right this instant. But she'd run a mile, it was written all over her.

'I can't help it, I'm a perfectionist and unfortunately I've decided to do something I'm lousy at. Makes a great combination.'

'Yet throw you into a life-threatening situation you've never dealt with before, like a bushfire, and you turn into Superwoman.'

'Silly, isn't it?' She was laughing. She hadn't taken offence. Another plus: she didn't take herself so seriously she couldn't be teased. 'Look.' She was pointing at a little stage set up at the front of the room where a woman was adjusting a microphone. 'The entertainment is about to begin. You might want to steel yourself. Betty is a serial offender—I mean, contender—at Monday night karaoke.'

Phoebe laughed as he exaggerated his shocked offence when Betty began to wail along to her chosen soundtrack.

'She fancies herself a latter-day Ella Fitzgerald.'

'Why hasn't someone put her out of her misery and told her how woeful she is?' He winced as if in pain. He was in pain! 'More than woeful.'

'She sets such a low benchmark it encourages many more people to get up there and have a go, and all money raised from the cover charge goes to charity so it's for a good cause. What's a few burst eardrums between friends?'

'Excruciatingly painful?' He moved his gaze from Betty to Phoebe. 'And you look just as much in pain when you are talking about your French lessons so why do it? And why, judging from what Ned said this morning, are you a serial course attendee?'

'French because I have a dream to go and live there and waft around a cottage in the hills making...' she paused '...goat's cheese or...or... shelling peas on my front stone steps. Or something.'

'Any particular reason why it's cheese and peas?'

She swatted him on the arm but the touch ended quickly. He was used to women draping themselves over him, pushing for physical contact. She wasn't like that and it made him want more.

She shrugged. 'I have a thing for fresh produce.' And for not telling the whole truth, he'd bet. There was more to her desire to go to France than just vegetables.

'The French men didn't factor into your decision?'

She jumped a little, her dark eyes widening. Why? 'No,' she said, repeating more forcefully, 'No.'

He'd been right this morning. Phoebe froze or startled when the words 'married' and 'men' were mentioned. What was that about? He'd find out before the night was out but confronting her wasn't the way.

'The other courses?' Judging by the way she relaxed her shoulders, which had noticeably hunched when he'd mentioned men, she was relieved he'd dropped the topic. 'Just how many are we talking about?'

'What's so subversive about taking a few

courses?' The light had returned to her eyes, she was smiling again, so they must be back on safe ground.

'A few?'

'All right, twenty or so, but why are we counting?' She was laughing again.

'Do you have a magic number in mind or do you plan to keep on going until you've run out of options?'

'Sooner or later I'll find something I love so much I can stop looking.'

She wasn't laughing any more. There was a shadowed hunger in her eyes and a sadness in her voice that told him she was talking about more than just courses. He sat quietly for a moment longer, watching her, giving her space to fill in the blanks if she chose.

She didn't.

Instead, Betty finished her song to muted applause and a few wolf-whistles to which Phoebe said, 'There are some merciful souls in the audience.'

'If they were merciful, they'd put her out of her misery.' He paused while he assessed the next female 'talent' to ascend the makeshift stage, catching Phoebe's eye and sharing a grin when it became clear the twenty-something girl was serenading, in a drunken fashion, Ned, who was paying scant attention, focussing instead on the woman half on his lap. 'What about you? Does Betty make you look talented?'

She shuddered. 'I'm musically challenged, too. Language and musical talent go together, right? Same cerebral hemisphere?'

'Everyone can learn to sing.' He held out a hand and she simply stared at him in horror. 'Let's give it a go.'

'Uh-uh. I don't believe for a second everyone can learn to sing.' Her eyes were huge, round and full of disbelief. It was clear what she was thinking: just how far was he going to push this?

'I don't believe it either but a doo-whop girl doesn't really need to sing. I'm sure you've got some moves hidden away somewhere. Come,' he said, standing and extending his hand again, 'be my doo-whop girl.'

'You want me to play your adoring sidekick? The big rock star's bit of fluff on the side?'

'It's great you think I'm a rock star when you haven't even seen my band. You're practically a groupie already.' He paused, considering, holding back a smile. 'Groupies make great doo-whop girls.'

She'd risen now, too, and slid out of the booth, facing him, her hands on her hips, her cheeks flushed, slightly breathless. 'You want to do a doo-whop number?' Her smile was pure sweetness and light and he didn't buy it for a second.

'With you. Absolutely.' He was laughing and she swatted him on the arm again, striding off through the small crowd to the far end of the room where the singer was half falling off the stage in her haste to stake her claim on Ned.

He followed at a slower pace, enjoying watching Phoebe as she spoke to the DJ. They were having an animated discussion. Phoebe was nodding her head vigorously and her smile was full of challenge as he joined her. She climbed up to the stage like a seasoned pro and grabbed the mike like she'd been born to the spotlight, not like a woman who five minutes ago had been protesting she couldn't sing. Her gaze zeroed in on him. What did she have up her sleeve?

'Ladies and gentlemen,' she began, and the crowd stamped their feet and treated her to plenty of wolf-whistles. 'I have an old classic for you tonight, but it wouldn't be as special without some help from my doo-whop boy.' More cheers from the crowd. And he knew now exactly what she had up that sleeve. 'Please give a warm welcome to Hahndorf's newest fireman, Max Williams!' She raised her voice to a shout, ending on a whoop that he'd never have seen coming.

The crowd cheered again, those who didn't know him—and that was most of them—craning to get a look at him as he saluted her, laughing, letting her know he'd meet her challenge.

One hand on the stage, he swung himself up next to her, slipping into performance mode as the opening strains of the music started, the tune immediately familiar, the words displayed on the small screen in front of them. Phoebe, laughter in her eyes, handed him a mike, and pointed for him to stand just behind her.

She didn't falter as the melody started, starting off a little nervously but quickly warming up. She wasn't really singing, it was more a full-throated crooning, half speaking, half singing, her way of getting around the need to actually sing. As the crowd got into her act and clapped and called her name, she started to move her body, too, and

Betty and whoever else had been on stage were made to look the amateurs they were.

The girl could move. So much so it took a wide-eyed look from her to remind him he was meant to be earning his keep as a doo-whop boy. Leaning in next to her, he delivered his back-up vocals, *de do run run run de do run run,* bringing more catcalls from the crowd and a split second of open-mouthed astonishment from Phoebe.

Whatever she'd been expecting, it wasn't his best falsetto, the high pitch of his voice as he did his best to be a doo-whop girl. Somehow they made it to the end of the song, Phoebe growling her way through her lyrics, Max not missing a beat with his female impersonation.

As the song ended, the crowd erupted into applause and Phoebe collapsed into laughter against his side as he held up her hand and made her take a bow, not releasing her hand as they left the stage. From the front row Ned was whistling, his fingers in his mouth, and making more racket than most of the room put together. Phoebe's hands were covering her flushed cheeks as she looked up into Max's eyes, for once not hiding anything, letting him see her surprise that she'd enjoyed it so much.

'That was an inspiring performance,' he said as they moved aside for an older gentleman to take to the stage.

'Thanks. I've never done anything like that before.'

'So I gathered,' he teased.

'Hey, be nice! Unless that *was* the nicest thing you can say, in which case be silent.'

'You were great.' He held up a hand to reinforce his sincerity. 'Really, much more entertaining than poor Betty. In actual fact, you were very good. I don't know why you made such a fuss about not wanting to do it.'

'You're incorrigible. I didn't make a fuss, I just didn't want to be your doo-whop girl.'

'You succeeded admirably on that front. Remind me never to have a battle of wits with you again. And by the way, where did you learn that terrific baritone growl? That really was impressive.'

'Although I could only ever dream of reaching those high notes you made look so...' She paused, searching for the word, laughing again. 'Um, effortless.'

He tipped an imaginary hat. 'Any time.' Glancing at the man on stage, who was singing a country ballad, he said, 'Finally something easy on the ears. Present company excepted, naturally.'

'Naturally.'

'Speaking of which, since you so thoroughly did me over on the doo-whop front, I'll buy the drinks. Same again?'

'Thanks.' She let her gaze linger on his retreating figure for a moment, until her attention was caught by Ned, who sent out another ear-splitting wolf-whistle for her benefit as he returned to their booth.

He called her back, patting the seat beside him for her to sit down. Phoebe greeted the two women who'd followed Ned there, receiving sulky glares in return, followed by an announce-ment they were off to the bar.

'You're out of favour now,' she said as they left, further demonstrating their irritation with the interruption by flouncing away. 'You really shouldn't play them so much.'

'Don't start. They know I'm not looking for anything serious. Is it my fault if they all seem to think they're the one who can help me change?' He was attempting to make a tower from the card-board coasters scattered across the table. 'Damn,' he muttered as it fell over before he could add a fourth coaster.

'If only they knew there was no knight in shining armour hiding deep beneath that uniform.'

'If it's knights and armour they want they should be looking at Max, not me.'

Phoebe looked over to the bar where Max was waiting for their drinks. He stood taller than most of the crowd and it wasn't difficult to imagine him rushing to the rescue. 'Is there something I should know?'

Ned grinned at her. 'Why? Are you interested?'

'No,' she said, even as she started to picture being swept off her feet into Max's gorgeous arms.

'Pity. I can just see the two of you galloping off into the sunset on a white stallion.'

'Now you're just being ridiculous. We've only just met and I won't be galloping off with anyone, as you well know.'

'So you won't mind that I've suggested to Max he stays on and we'll see how he works out as the third housemate?'

'What?'

'We've talked about having a third person in the house. We're both trying to save money and I thought Max was a good choice. You'll get to France that much quicker if we can cut our rent. Although why you insist on paying rent when it's your parents' place…' He shrugged, not completing his sentence as he started another tower of coasters.

'It's your parents' place?' Max slid into one of the chairs at the end of the booth, handing out the drinks. Phoebe hadn't noticed him returning—had he heard her vehement 'What?'? He didn't appear offended or embarrassed, so perhaps not.

'They own the property it's on.' She stopped speaking as another singer began, smiling at Max as they both breathed a sigh of relief that this woman could hold a tune, although her delivery was lifeless. 'And…' she turned back to Ned '…I pay rent because I'm twenty-nine years old and I don't think I should be living off my parents.'

'Where do they live?' Max asked as he picked up his beer and clinked his glass against hers before taking a sip.

'On the property as well, but in a new house they built. It was always Mum's dream to retire to somewhere green.'

'They're not from here originally?'

She shook her head. 'Sydney, and then they lived for years in Broken Hill for Dad's work—he's in the mining industry.'

'Heat and red dust weren't your mum's idea of heaven?'

'She bore it with grace.' Phoebe chuckled. 'But I think it was in the small print of their marriage contract that one day they'd move somewhere like this.'

'It's beautiful,' said Max, looking at her, holding her gaze even though she was telling herself to break it, to look away, to pretend to be interested in Ned's coaster building. He was talking about her! And he'd think she was interested in *him* if she didn't look somewhere else but, well, she couldn't. Not when he was looking at her like she was amazing, a thought that trickled syrupy feelings right into her tingling toes.

'We had some…' She hesitated as she seemed to choose her words carefully. 'Things happen. I moved here to be closer to Mum and Dad.'

'And now? Is everything OK?' Once again, just like at the scene of the car accident, Phoebe truly felt as though Max had her best interests at heart.

She felt sure it wasn't idle curiosity making him ask the question.

'You won't find yourself caught up in a soap-opera drama if you move in.' She nodded, hating herself for lying when he was being so considerate, but not able to tell him the whole truth either. Besides, things were better, even if they still weren't perfect. She'd been stripped of any expectations that there was such a thing as a perfect life. 'You're quite safe.'

'So you're OK with me moving in?'

'It's fine.' Although the way her stomach pitched as she said it suggested she was nervous. 'There's plenty of room and we're all doing shift work, we'll probably barely see each other.' Who was she trying to convince?

'I'll be the perfect housemate,' he said as he drew a cross across his chest.

'We're counting on it,' Ned interjected as he attempted to place another coaster on the stack. Phoebe had almost forgotten he was there she'd been so focussed on Max.

Ned's tower collapsed again and with his expletive the moment was broken. No surprises there. Tower-building clearly wasn't his strong point.

She laughed to herself and Max was grinning, too, a shared joke just between the two of them.

'Mate, such high feats of engineering should be left to the experts. I'll put you out of your misery.'

Ned snorted and shoved the fallen coasters over to Max, folding his arms across his chest and leaning back in his chair as though disinterested in the outcome. But he was watching Max's movements like a hawk. 'He thinks he's a whiz just because he studied civil engineering.'

'You did?' She never would have picked him for the type to spend years at university. He seemed much more of a free spirit.

Max nodded, concentrating on the coasters, which were now at the third tier, earning a derisive snort from Ned.

'You didn't like it?'

Max took a moment to answer. He was placing his last coaster to make a roof on the tower, now four levels in all, Ned coughing loudly just as Max lifted his hand away, but Max didn't flinch. The tower held and Phoebe chuckled at the look of satisfaction on Max's face and sulky defeat on Ned's.

Ned drained his drink. 'I'm going to go stand at the bar and wait for a woman.'

'Neanderthal,' said Phoebe with fondness as she waved him off. 'Don't engineers have a reputation as beer-drinking neanderthals?'

'Which is why I am not an engineer.'

'Really?'

'That, and I failed third year.' He was grinning and although she was woefully out of the loop when it came to men, she'd still swear there was a look of appreciation in his eyes. And not much concern about his failure to graduate from university. 'Or rather I chose not to pass.'

'You didn't like it?'

'Got it in one. Put it down to the inexperience of youth and the abject terror with which I regarded my mother at that age and you have the full story of why I did engineering in the first place.'

'You have a scary mother?'

'Terrifying. But fortunately no longer to me. I think she's come round to the idea that I'll be a perpetual disappointment to her.'

'She doesn't approve of you being a firefighter?'

'It's the music, darling,' he said, mimicking his mother in a way that told Phoebe he was, despite her shortcomings, very fond of her. 'It's not a way to better oneself. She couldn't understand why I'd give up status and wealth in order to have job satisfaction. But there are plenty of things more important than money.'

'Maybe she had visions of you never being able to afford to move out of home.'

'The eternal lodger?' He nodded, the corners of his eyes creasing up with his smile as he shook his head. 'I didn't fulfil her fears on that score, then. Hanging about the family nest was never going to be me, but she'd still prefer me to have a degree in something—anything! She'd *love* you, Phoebe. With all those courses you do, you'd qualify as the "right sort of person."' He roared with laughter at the expression of anxiety she hadn't been quick enough to hide. 'I'm not about to drag you home for Christmas dinner so stop panicking. But…' he stood up and bent back down until his lips were an inch or so from her ear '…there's no one at the mike now and I'm going to sing. If I win, I hear there's a prize of dinner at the hotel and I hear they do a mean line in baritone-sized burgers, just right for you. So I'll let you off family dinner if you have dinner with me.'

'You're mighty confident for a man who has a higher vocal range than most women.'

'You're not sounding like that groupie I ordered,' he said with a wink before he disappeared to the stage, leaving her wondering just what he'd think of her if he knew the truth about her. Her old job. Her old pay packet. Her old life, period.

He was living his dream, whereas she'd had hers and hadn't taken enough care of it. But she wasn't about to spill those beans tonight. Or any night. She put her past from her mind and let herself be swept away by his charisma, just as the crowd was doing. He was on stage, belting out a classic rock number that had the crowd on their feet, clapping along and joining in at the chorus as if they were at a concert.

He could move.

He could sing.

And from the way he was looking at her, he was doing it all just for her.

And she knew that if she saw him singing that way to anyone else, she'd be devastated. Which made no sense at all unless…

'Oh, dear,' she muttered, as Ned returned to the table with two new women in tow, who vied with each other to see who could sit closer to Ned, although Phoebe saw one of them was also casting appreciative glances at Max.

'What?'

'I've become a groupie. At the ripe old age of twenty-nine I've fallen for a rock star.'

'I'll drink to that.' He did just that, raising his beer glass in a toast. 'I'll see if I can get a poster of him for your bedroom wall.'

Phoebe didn't answer. She was only half-aware of Ned or anyone else even being there, so focussed was she on Max. He was building his song to a big ending and the crowd was lapping it up, although every note he sang was sung to her, seeking out her gaze with no apology for doing so, no fear he'd be rejected.

And she was aware, too, that something crazy had just happened.

For a brief moment—how long was a song? Two minutes? Three?—she'd fallen under the spell of one very charismatic man and imagined herself in a world where she was free to do just that.

But imagining was the active word here. She came to her senses as Max finished and saluted the crowd in thanks for their applause.

She wasn't free. Not to imagine and not to get involved.

The DJ was back at the mike, motioning for

Max to stay with him on stage as he said, 'All right folks, that was the last song for the night and it's time to announce this week's winner from our three crowd favourites. John "Kenny Rogers" Paech, Vanessa aka "Beyonce", come on up and join Max the Fireman!'

The crowd erupted as the three best acts of the evening were reunited on stage and the DJ revved them up further. 'There can only be one winner and you get to decide who that will be. The biggest round of applause will determine the lucky performer so, ladies and gentlemen, let's hear it for "Kenny"!'

There was better than polite applause for 'Kenny', who'd sung the country ballad. She hadn't stayed until this time before, she'd always been happy to head home earlier than Ned. Essential, really, since by the time she left, Ned had at least one woman hanging on his every word, making it clear she was eager to leave with him. This time, though, she was enjoying it, enjoying the rowdiness of the crowd. No doubt the DJ was introducing the acts in order of good to better, knowing the crowd would get louder with each introduction so it was no surprise when

Beyonce got louder applause than Kenny. And no surprise again that when Max stepped forward, the crowd's cheers dwarfed the previous responses. Wolf-whistles, clapping, banging of palms and glasses on tables. Max was the clear crowd favourite. Why wouldn't he be? He was that rare sort of man the men all wanted to be like—and the women all wanted to be with.

Grinning, he stepped forward to shake the DJ's and the other contestants' hands, accepting his prize with good humour.

'Thanks everyone, thanks, Kenny, Beyonce,' he said, nodding at his competition. And then, searching her out, his gaze found hers and locked as he said, 'This one's for you, Phoebe.' Holding the envelope with his prize aloft, his voice holding promises she found she desperately wanted him to keep, he added, 'We officially have a date.'

Max handed back the microphone and jumped off the stage, skirting the crowd, refusing to be waylaid as he made a beeline for her. Every nerve in her body was alive with anticipation. They were both thinking of re-creating the lost moment yesterday, she knew it. Yet the nerves she would have expected didn't appear nor did all her sensible arguments about why this couldn't happen. All she felt was a wonderful sensation, a feeling she was about to experience something delicious, something she hadn't thought would be coming her way for a long time, if ever.

Max didn't hesitate when he reached her, simply gathered her into his arms in one deliberate movement, literally sweeping her off her feet. She didn't resist, she couldn't have even if she'd wanted to. Her body was too busy responding to his touch. With one hand he was holding her at her waist, his touch firm. His other hand was at her shoulder, his thumb reaching to the back of her neck, and little shivers coursed down her spine. She had one foot off the floor, which threw her off balance, making it natural for her to hold on to Max's arms for support, aware of his taut muscles under her hands, aware that her fingers could barely span half his upper arms.

She tipped her head back, meeting his gaze. He was looking very pleased with the situation, his dark eyes full of mischief and something else, too—desire?

'So we have date.'

It wasn't a question, which was fortunate as

she was incapable of formulating an answer. Her brain was far too occupied processing the myriad sensations sliding over her skin. She nodded anyway, but she knew the nod was not in response to his statement—it was a sign that she wanted him to kiss her. No, hang wanting! This was a need: she *needed* to have this consuming urgency coursing through her body satisfied or she'd go quietly insane. Or not so quietly?

He bent his head to hers, his breath warm and sweet. She closed her eyes, savouring the moment, knowing even the simple fact she was in Max's arms was nothing short of miraculous.

Then he kissed her.

And she experienced her second miracle of the evening.

CHAPTER FIVE

GRANTED, the kiss was over in a flash. Her lips had parted in response to the pressure from Max's but before she could react completely, he'd pulled away, easing her back onto her feet. It was all over in a moment, but her reaction wasn't. Luckily, he was still holding her or she would have collapsed on the spot. It was just a kiss, she told herself, yet it left her feeling breathless and disoriented.

The crowd around them had disappeared from her consciousness until, in her mind, it was just the two of them, suspended in time. Now, as she became aware of the noise and activity around them, she wanted everyone to disappear again. No, who was she kidding? She wouldn't care how many people there were if he'd just kiss her. Now! She stood silent, encircled by his arms, waiting. She could hear him breathing, was mesmerised by the sight of his chest rising and falling. She looked up at him and the heat and passion in his eyes took her breath away. Whatever it was that was happening between them, he felt it as much as she did.

'Well done, mate.' Ned was clapping him on the shoulder, jostling him, jostling Phoebe, too. 'A solid debut performance at karaoke night,' Ned added, and Phoebe exhaled the breath of panic she'd held when she'd thought Ned had been congratulating Max on kissing her. Which would have been nonsensical. Ned wouldn't do that, proving to her how shaken she was.

Max was chatting easily to Ned. He didn't seem unsettled, let alone rattled, like she was, and he'd dropped his arm from about her. Had she imagined he was as affected by her as she was by him?

'It's last drinks—can I get you both something to celebrate? Phoebes, champagne?' Ned didn't appear to think anything unusual was happening but Phoebe's heart was still racing and her breathing was shallow. Champagne was not what she needed right now.

'I'm fine, thanks, Ned, it's probably time I went

home.' She answered Ned but her gaze kept returning to Max.

'I'll drive your car home, Phoebe. I got a lift here with Ned.'

'Good idea, guys. I'll catch you later.'

'Ned seems all in favour.' Max laughed as they watched him disappear with his arm around one of the girls. Phoebe couldn't remember what the girl's name was, she just hoped Ned could.

Max grabbed their jackets from the booth as Phoebe searched through her bag for her car keys.

'I don't mind driving,' she said when she saw Max holding his hand out, waiting for the keys.

'How many drinks have you had?'

'I don't remember.'

'In that case, I don't think you should drive.' His fingers brushed her palm as he took the keys, sending more shivers down her spine. She let go of the keys without protest, the tingles of anticipation hijacking her thought processes.

Max held the door open for her as they left the pub and she was hit with a blast of cold, fresh air, a stark contrast to the stale air inside. Away from the noise of the crowd Phoebe was suddenly aware her head wasn't as clear as she'd thought.

Those unaccustomed drinks had done the trick on her empty stomach. She was happy to slide into the passenger seat.

'Had a good night?' Max asked as he started the car. There was no sign of awkwardness, no sign he'd kissed her less than ten minutes ago. He was so together, whereas her head was a wild, zig-zagging jumble of thoughts, all centred on the man sitting next to her, oh, so cool and collected.

'More than I've had in a long time,' Phoebe answered, managing to squelch the give-away tremor in her voice. Just.

'You were a natural with the mike.'

'More natural without it.' The memory of his falsetto voice melted her reserve and she laughed. 'I'm not nearly the born showman you clearly are.' Glancing his way, she took in the strong profile, his relaxed posture as he lightly held the steering-wheel. Could she? Should she? She said a quick prayer that she wouldn't sound foolish and plunged in. 'Speaking of which, I'd really like to come and see your band someday. Ned says you do originals and the band is really good.' She blurted it out then held her breath.

'You'll be waiting a while.' He turned the car

onto the dirt driveway that led past her parents' place and then on to their cottage. 'Our drummer is away so we don't have another gig lined up for a month, but you're very welcome then. In the meantime, we're concentrating on getting the mix right for the next CD.'

'You record?' He seemed to think it was perfectly reasonable she'd suggested coming to see him play.

'Are you telling me Ned doesn't have us on repeat at home?'

'Afraid not, but I'd like to hear.'

'I hope you mean that, because a muso only needs to be asked once,' he laughed, as he stopped the car.

Walking beside him to the front door, she may as well have been drifting in the ether. She'd overcome her now ever-present reserve and suggested going to see him play and he hadn't seemed to think she'd made a spectacle of herself. What's more, the world hadn't ground to a halt.

Then they reached the door and at the same time both saw the large yellow envelope lying on the doormat. The feeling of wafting about on clouds evaporated immediately.

'What's that?'

It was addressed to her, care of her parents', the

sender's address printed in the top left-hand corner. She picked it up, she knew what it was.

'A letter from my lawyers. Dad must have dropped it off for me.'

Max still held her keys. He found the house key and unlocked the front door, then followed her to the kitchen where she dropped the letter on the table before flicking the kettle on.

'Not keen to know what's in it?'

Phoebe glanced at the envelope warily, as if she was afraid it might open itself. 'It's just a new copy of my will.'

'How can you be so sure? Maybe someone's left you a huge inheritance.'

She laughed. 'I doubt that very much. I'm not known for being a lucky person. I've just changed my will, making Mum and Dad my beneficiaries.'

'Who was it before?'

'My husband.' Phoebe froze as the words left her mouth. What on earth had possessed her to tell him that? Damn those drinks!

Or should she blame her subconscious? Her hormones had been sent into overdrive following Max's kiss and she couldn't pretend she wasn't slightly terrified about what might happen next between them.

'You're married.'

She cringed. 'Sort of.' How would she get out of this?

'Sort of?' The only word for his expression was grim. 'How does that work?'

'We're separated.'

He'd done it again. He cursed his damn fool luck under his breath. How had he managed to get involved again with someone with complications? Where were the simple women? He knew the answer to that question. They were the type of girls Ned went home with, fun for a night or two but not interesting enough for him. He'd never been one for brief relationships and lately not for any relationships at all, which had made this sudden, unlooked-for attraction to Phoebe as surprising as it had been enjoyable. He liked interesting women but the older he got the more he found that interesting and complicated were often combined. And he could do without complications.

It explained the tension this morning when Ned

had mentioned the word married but what, exactly, did it mean now? And was that the source of the family drama Phoebe had talked about? He'd just assumed it had had something to do with her parents but he'd based that on absolutely nothing.

'Is it a trial separation or something more permanent?' He looked at her ring finger as he asked the question, a reflex, even though he knew that finger was bare.

'Pretty permanent. The divorce is just about through. Soon I'll be filling out "divorcee" on paperwork. I hate that word.'

Max disagreed. 'Divorcee' sounded much better than 'married' when he thought about Phoebe.

He'd never had a relationship with a married woman and he wasn't about to start now. But what was he wanting to start anyway? He hadn't thought that far, he'd just been enjoying getting to know her, enjoying the fact she'd seemed keen not to rush into something serious. And now he knew why she'd be reluctant. He just didn't know what that meant for him.

She was pouring their coffee as though it really did take all her concentration and was not just a stalling tactic. Then again, she did remember he had milk and two sugars so perhaps she was interested. His spirits were unexpectedly buoyed by that small fact. Nonsensical, he knew. He had no idea what his intentions were regarding her. What did he care if she thought he took his coffee cold, black and as bitter as they came?

But he did care, at some level. If he didn't, he wouldn't have picked up on any of this. And because he cared, he needed to know what had gone wrong with her marriage. He'd made the same mistake once before by not asking Lisbette enough questions, or not asking the right questions, and it had come back to bite him.

But now was not the time. Phoebe was tired and a little the worse for wear. What she needed was to go to bed. By herself and with a big glass of water by her side. He'd leave his questions for another day.

He took the mug from her as she held it out. Neither of them had spoken again. She seemed lost in her thoughts and he sensed they weren't about him. He didn't like the feeling.

She picked up her mug and the yellow envelope and headed for her room, alone, and he couldn't deny his disappointment, even though he'd swear he hadn't brought her home tonight with any expectations.

'See you tomorrow,' Max said as she said good-night and left the kitchen.

Their paths probably wouldn't cross, but he said it anyway. Phoebe had the day off. He was getting together with the band straight after his shift to work on the CD mix and wouldn't be back until well after midnight.

His questions would wait. Patience was apparently a virtue, and in this case rushing things wasn't the way to go. Despite the sparks they were generating, a gentle approach was required. She'd built a hard outer shell—a protective measure?—and it would take time for him to get beyond that. No doubt her failed marriage had contributed to it and he didn't want to risk making her armour more impenetrable by rushing things. Sparks were easily extinguished and he suspected Phoebe would have all sorts of measures at her disposal to do just that. A slow approach, keeping things burning gently, was a better way of building a fire that would last.

The thought surprised him. As he sat in the kitchen, slowly spinning his cup in front of him on the bench, the ticking of the wall clock and the low whirr of the old fridge the only background noises for his musings, he wondered if he could mean it. Could he really be thinking of getting involved at all, let alone with someone he'd just met? If he was, it would be the first time since he'd left Canada with his ego and his faith in women similarly bruised. So maybe she had made him think that way again, but what he didn't know was whether he could trust his instincts anymore. They'd been so off the wall with Lisbette.

He sat and pondered the possibilities, watching the liquid in his mug, the swirling milky darkness of the coffee a reflection of the confusing whirl-pool in his mind.

Phoebe was in the duty office, scanning her emails as they popped up in her inbox. One stood out. It was from Max, whom she hadn't seen since Monday night when she'd found 'the envelope' that had made her hastily throw up a wall between them.

She'd talked herself over her horror after blurting out her past. It wasn't the end of the world, she'd told herself. Lots of people were divorced and she didn't have to tell him the whole story. She'd even caught herself looking for signs of Max as she'd gone about the house. Now she was at work, she was doing the same, and hoping this email would be personal, not work related.

Clicking on the email, she saw her name was only one in a long list of all staff. Not personal, then.

Max was looking for paramedics who'd be interested in doing a PR visit to the local primary school and kindergarten. He explained that since the bushfire a number of children were edgy when they heard sirens. The fire department thought a visit letting the children experience the fire engines and ambulances would help allay fears.

Phoebe had been involved in these exercises before. They were run quite regularly through the school year and the kids always loved the chance to peer inside the ambulance. She assumed they'd be just as excited, if not more so, with the chance to climb inside a fire engine. She sent back her reply. Of course she'd go.

A minute later Max was in the duty office too, deep in conversation with Cookie.

Chancing a few glances, she remembered all over again why he was so appealing. It was more than his physical attributes, considerable as they were. He made her feel hopeful. He was expectation and anticipation all rolled into one gorgeous package.

For so long all she'd felt had been a duty to get through the day. Her plans for the future had been lost with Joe. And the end of her marriage had left her with nothing but a suddenly useless medical degree, a career as a paramedic and her parents' emotional support. And a few new, well-chosen friends like Ned.

Her main prerequisite for new friends was people who knew how to mind their own business. It explained why her new friends were all men: they didn't dig down into uncomfortable places in the name of emotional connection.

Old friends had gone the way of her old life. One way or another, she'd left it all behind.

Sure, she was fortunate to have what she still did but she'd dreamt and planned for much more. But the pain of the past three years had changed her plans and now she only lived in the short term. Looking into the future, seeing a longer-term future, was no longer an option. She had no idea what her future held and didn't want to guess. Surprises were overrated.

Now, though, she recognised what Max represented. He made her feel safe, he made her laugh. She was attracted to him and it all gave her hope her future might not be quite as bleak as she'd learned to accept. Max might not be part of her future but the simple fact she'd started thinking positively again since meeting him could only be a good thing.

Max made her feel alive when for so long a dark part of her—deep down, hidden from everyone and mostly even from herself—had felt otherwise.

He made his way to her side, her spirits lifting with every step he took. He pulled up a chair, swinging it around and sitting on it with his elbows resting on the back. 'Good day?'

'Quiet.' She nodded at the screen. 'Hence the email checking. Do you have the details for the kindergarten visit yet?' She didn't want to gabble on, but the last time she'd seen him, he'd just given her an unforgettable kiss then she'd blurted out she was getting divorced. Getting a handle on her nerves was imperative if she didn't want to risk being oh so smooth again. Logging off, she couldn't avoid eye contact any more and she turned to him. Would he see in her face how much she'd been fantasising about his kisses?

If he did, he didn't let on. 'You've put your name down?'

She nodded and saw the approval in his eyes. Did she come across as that much of a loner that he'd doubted she'd get involved? 'I've done them before, but never in response to an event like a bushfire and never jointly with the fire service. It's always been a goodwill thing, not a real need to help calm children's fears.'

'And…,' he winked at her, his smile warming her down to her toes '…the hero-worship is always good for the ego.'

'I think I chose the wrong emergency service.' She glanced around to see if anyone was watching but it was clear they were attracting no attention. Everyone else seemed focussed on their tasks, so she relaxed into the conversation. Max was laid-back, showing no sign of awkwardness, and it helped her do the same, especially knowing she wasn't under scrutiny. 'We paramedics all but get bowled over as the children make a rush for the ambulance. If they didn't eventually realise they need us to show them what things are, we wouldn't get a second glance.'

'I doubt that very much.' His words were sincere but the light in his eyes made the *double entendre* clear. 'Although, I agree, firefighters get better press than ambos. There's no animated children's TV series or Hollywood blockbusters about you people in green.' He puffed up his chest with mock self-importance.

'Luckily it's all so realistic,' she said, surprising herself that, despite her nerves about seeming awkward or out of touch with him, it didn't take long in his company for her to feel at ease.

He winked at her. 'If a scriptwriter saw you, I think there'd at least be a documentary about ambos starring Phoebe Wilson.'

She shrugged, embarrassed and pleased at the same time and pleased all over again when he said, 'Are we on for dinner tonight?'

Pleased she may be, but free she was not. 'I can't tonight.' She hesitated. She was having dinner with her parents and Ned would often tag along for a home-cooked meal and to flirt with her mum and talk about farm stuff with her dad. Early on, her parents had hoped Ned might be the one to bring back the Phoebe they knew, but time had convinced them he was too much of a larrikin to be a safe bet for their bruised and damaged daughter.

So the question was, should she? Shouldn't she? Etiquette on leaving out a housemate warred with the wisdom of inviting a man she'd only just met, one she'd already kissed, to meet her parents.

'From your frown, I take it it's an appointment you could do without. Want me to text you with an emergency call half an hour into it?'

'It's not that. It's dinner with my parents, but I was just—' She broke off. Was she crazy, about to confide her quandary over him *to* him?

'You were just wondering how to tell me Ned's invited and I'm not.' His grin was full of the rogue element that had so wowed her on stage two nights ago. He was totally irresistible. He'd have been winding women around his finger since he'd been a toddler.

'You knew when you invited me to dinner that I was busy?' Once again he'd lifted her over the hurdle of her embarrassment with his teasing— and his ability to apparently read her mind. 'You're a shocker, nothing like the gentleman you pretend to be,' she said, but her voice was devoid of chiding.

'I'll admit to ulterior motives. Ned raves about your mum's country roasts, and as my mum has only been known to home-cook twice since I was born, it's the sort of treat I'm prepared to go to great lengths to get my hands on.'

She opened her mouth to speak but quite simply wasn't sure what to say. Her mum and dad wouldn't mind. On the contrary, they loved crowds of people as much as their daughter did not. But was this moving too fast or was this simply a case of the new housemate coming to dinner?

'And I'll come clean to put you out of your misery. As long as you're only concerned about having to impose on your parents on my behalf, there's no need to worry. I bumped into your parents this morning on my way in with Ned and once we'd helped your dad load up his trailer, your mum insisted on Ned and I both coming to dinner.'

'Meaning Mum took one look at you and decided you needed fattening up?' She wasn't sure how she felt about that, but she'd been right when she'd thought Max had been wrapping women around his little finger since his birth. Men, too, apparently. What she'd give to have that relaxed air of confidence, that aura exuding natural charm. Whatever she'd once had of that had deserted her a few years back. 'Your groupies won't like a tubby rocker.'

He sent her one of his trade-mark winks. 'My groupies are well satisfied.'

The station bells sounded and they fell silent to hear the announcement.

'Attention, attention, 261 and 264 responding to a house fire in Mt Barker.'

'I've got to run but we're on? Dinner with your parents?'

'Just go save people and houses.' She waved him away good-naturedly. 'And don't hog all the gravy tonight.'

'You've got it.' He gave her shoulder a gentle squeeze in response and then was gone, leaving her discreetly resting her fingers on the spot his had just been.

Stomach flutters, karaoke serenading, kisses and now dinner with her parents.

Where was this headed?

It was a scary question.

The thought this might be headed nowhere, that this was nothing more than a holiday fling for Max, was scarier still.

There was no point skirting around the issue: she was falling for him.

No, the past tense was needed here. She'd fallen for him.

So did that mean the impossible might be possible after all? Could her future hold more than simply a life spent trying to forget?

Max kicked off his shoes and stepped into his fire boots and overalls, pulling the straps over his shoulders then swinging himself into the cab of 261 with Ned, Mitch and Tiny, who was, predictably, huge.

Ned had the engine running and as soon as the station doors were up he pulled out, turning left towards the freeway. Cookie and his crew followed in 264. Max knew that being called to a fire in Mt Barker meant they wouldn't be the first response but it was still his job to get the details and keep his team informed and safe. He hit the buttons on the mobile data terminal, sending a signal back to the station confirming they were on the road then read the directions and address off the screen so Mitch could check the map and direct Ned as they approached Mt Barker.

'You get the green light?' Ned had waited until they were on the freeway before asking the question. He was being—for him—discreet, not mentioning Phoebe by name, but Max knew what he was talking about.

'By default. Not sure how to read it.'

'Hang in there, buddy.'

They left it at that, their concentration turning to the job.

The police had barricaded both ends of the street and two officers were keeping spectators at bay, but they dragged the barriers to one side as Ned approached.

Looking at the scene, Max didn't doubt they'd be put to work. Ned switched off the siren and pulled the fire engine to the side of the street. Max hit the buttons on the MDT, letting Hahndorf know they'd arrived at the scene. In front of them was a row of attached cottages, smoke billowing from their roofs.

The police hadn't been completely successful at keeping people away but fortunately they had been herded together on the opposite side of the road, although, in Max's opinion, that was still too close. He certainly wouldn't choose to be near a burning building if he wasn't working. Plenty of hills' houses used LPG gas and it didn't take much for those tanks to explode.

'Suit up, guys, while I find the IC.'

The Incident Controller was easy to spot. Like Max, he was wearing a yellow helmet, signifying the rank of Station Officer, and he was juggling a handful of walkie-talkies. He'd seen Max and his crew arrive and waved Max over.

'Fire started in the middle cottage. There were reports of an explosion but no one seems to know whether the explosion came first or only after the fire had taken hold. We're working on containing the fire from the northern side but we could use a hand. Between your two crews can you take care of containment from the southern side and organise a search and rescue through the last house on that end?' He indicated the cottage on the southern end. 'Can I make you sector commander out the back of the houses?'

'Sure.'

'You can get access past that last one.' He handed Max a walkie-talkie. 'You can get me on 115.'

Max hurried back to the two appliances from Hahndorf. The crews were suited up, breathing apparatus on their backs, jackets over the top. Ned and Nifty had the hoses rolled out, Nifty was hooking them up to the pumps and Ned was organising the BA control board.

'Cookie, I need your crew on search and rescue in the southern cottage. My crew will work on containment from that end. I'll be round the back, co-ordinating things from there.'

Tiny and Mitch dropped their tags from their BA gear, pulled their flash hoods down, positioned their masks and helmets and went in through the front door, dragging the hoses behind them.

Max waited until they'd disappeared from view before making his way round to the back of the row cottages. The back gardens were separated by low fences and most of the yards had small lawn areas with a patio coming off the back of each house. Max stepped over the fences and positioned himself in the middle yard of the five cottages. He put a call in to the incident controller, letting him know he was in position and got a warning in return.

'The fire is spreading through the roof spaces. Need to stop the spread from that direction. Over.'

Max knew most of these old houses didn't have

fire walls extending up to the roof, making it too easy for the fire to take hold in the roof timbers and spread that way. His crew would need to pull the ceiling down to get at the fire.

'Portable 261 to Appliance 261. Ned, you there? Over.'

'Appliance 261. What is it, Max? Over?'

'I need a ceiling hook—can you bring it round? Over.'

'On the way. Over.'

Max scouted around, looking for any hazardous materials, wanting to assess the lie of the land as he waited for Ned. A figure moving in his peripheral vision made him turn his head. But it wasn't Ned. It was a young male, maybe around twenty years old and of scruffy appearance, and he was climbing over the fence into the yard where Max stood. Once he was over he started towards the burning cottage.

'Hey, what do you think you're doing?' Max called out to him, and the youth hesitated but didn't stop. He looked edgy, his eyes darting left and right as if gauging Max's position in relation to wherever it was he wanted to go.

'My stuff's in there. I need to get into the house.'

What planet was he on? 'Mate, it's on fire!'

It was madness to think of entering but Max had a sinking feeling this lad wasn't interested in reason. Max took a step forward, planning on putting himself between the youth and the house, but before he could block the path completely, the young man had darted around him and disappeared into the house.

'Damn it.' Max had to don his BA mask, plus his helmet, before he could follow. He couldn't let a civilian, even a really stupid one, which this one clearly was, run into a burning building. He threw his BA tag onto the ground where Ned was likely to find it and followed inside.

The house he entered was the origin of the fire and had been left to burn while the fire crews tried to contain the spread into the other houses. Thick smoke choked the rooms and the youth had a ten-second advantage. Ten seconds didn't sound like a lot but in a burning house, full of smoke, it complicated matters.

Max stayed as low to the ground as possible, trying to get beneath the smoke, but it didn't help. Visibility was nil.

He'd only gone a few steps when he crashed

into the corner of what he thought must be a kitchen table. Cursing, he felt his way around that and found the passage door. The kid had another advantage: he knew the layout of the house. Max kept his hand on the passage wall. Five paces along the passage he tripped and stumbled. It took him a second to realise he'd tripped over the lad, who must have stumbled and fallen himself.

Regaining his footing, he grabbed him by the shirt collar to drag him back through the house, but the lad wasn't having a bar of that. Kicking out at Max, he connected with his leg and Max felt a dull thud as his left calf muscle took a blow. It wasn't enough to topple him but it was enough to enable the youth to wriggle out of his grip. Staggering to his feet, the young man lashed out again as he tried to skirt Max's bulk. On reflex, Max stuck out his left foot and tripped him, pain shooting through his calf muscle as the youth collided with his leg. It was all happening so fast, and they were both reacting blindly in the smoke, but as he fell Max grabbed him again.

The smoke was working in Max's favour now and the lad was coughing and losing the energy to resist. He didn't have long before the youth would be overcome by fumes. He had to get him out. He dragged him down the passage, limping as he pulled him back through the kitchen. The extra effort was depleting his own oxygen supply and the ache in his left calf intensified each time he took his weight on that side.

Emerging from the building, he collapsed on the ground at Ned's feet.

Holding out the walkie-talkie given to him by the incident controller was all he needed to do. Ned took one look and got on the radio, calling for the paramedics and police to be sent around. Now.

Phoebe and Steve, like Max's fire crew, had been called to the scene as back-up. Unlike the other teams, they weren't engaged in treating anyone when the incident controller took the call. Not knowing what was required, they grabbed the oxygen cylinders and raced around to the back of the burning buildings.

Max was half lying, half sitting on the ground and Ned was next to him, kneeling beside a third figure, who had been rolled into the coma position.

'Ned, Max. What's happening?'

'This clown ran into a burning building. Max dragged him out. He needs treatment for smoke inhalation.'

'And, Max, what happened to you? Are you okay?'

'I'm fine, Phoebe.'

Something wasn't right but Phoebe couldn't put her finger on it. Max was conscious and seemed to be in one piece but her sixth sense was picking up a strange vibe. But Max had said he was fine and this young man lying by her feet obviously needed attention. Steve had started treatment, slipping a mask over the youth's face and running oxygen. Phoebe needed to catch up. She checked his oxygen sats as Steve began checking for any other injuries.

The police arrived and Phoebe was aware of Ned and Max telling their version of events. With a quick backward glance at Max, her intuition still working overtime, she dashed back to the ambulance to grab the stretcher.

Max was still sitting on the ground when she came back. Now she knew something wasn't right. She may not know him all that well but she was positive he wouldn't be lying around if he could possibly be upright.

The young man had recovered his wits with the hit of oxygen and was becoming obnoxious, enabling Steve to declare him fit to be moved. Phoebe was relieved when the police took him off their hands and away for questioning, leaving her free to focus on the casualty she was much more concerned about.

She knelt down next to Max, who was now looking pale. 'What happened?'

'The idiot stabbed me.'

CHAPTER SIX

HE'D be fine—her training reassured her of that straight away—but a cold wave of fear still washed over her because what if he *wasn't* OK?

Her rising panic told her she'd be losing more than a new housemate or more than a potential new friend. She'd be losing the only chance she'd had in three years at starting over.

Before now, she hadn't thought that was an option. Now she'd met Max, and a wilted part of her had stirred to life again. She wanted more, even though it was a chance she didn't deserve.

But what if it was offered anyway?

Stop the histrionics, she told herself, even though her train of thought had taken only a few seconds.

She focussed on Max. He was talking coherently. He had no signs of shock. He was sitting up, his left leg bent at the knee, and he had his hands clasped around his left calf. So what she needed to do was get on with checking him, get on with doing her job. She steadied herself where she squatted on the ground. 'I need to see.'

Max lifted his hands. They were bloodied but not bleeding. 'It's only a nick but it hurts to bear weight.'

Moving to his left side, she saw the leg of his overalls was torn and stained with blood. 'Only a nick?' Phoebe queried, eyebrows raised.

'I've had worse.'

'Will you be right?' Ned asked. 'I'd better get back on the job.'

'We'll be right.' Max answered him. 'Take this radio,' he said, holding it out. 'You'll have to co-ordinate the crews.'

'Sure thing.'

Ned and Steve were both gone now, and she was alone with Max.

She held his wrist, taking his pulse, hoping he wouldn't notice the tremor in her hand. 'Can you pull your trouser leg up so I can see the wound?'

He shook his head. 'Can't get them up far enough. I'll have to pull them down.' Ripping open the Velcro closures on his jacket, he slipped his arms out before pushing the straps of his overalls off his shoulders—not without difficulty, but he didn't ask for help so she held back. He was wearing a dark blue T-shirt under his jacket, a very snugly fitting T-shirt that hugged his shoulder and arm muscles rather too nicely. He lifted his weight off the ground, using his right leg, and slid his overalls past his hips.

What was he wearing under his overalls?

Trousers. Long, navy trousers. Long trousers—she could handle that, except they were coming off, too!

He undid the trousers and pushed them down as well, exposing boxer shorts and tanned, muscled legs. This was the part where she reminded herself she was a professional and Max was a patient.

She needed more than one reminder. Having been fully clad in protective gear, now he was in nothing but a T-shirt and boxers, his trousers bunched up at his feet, which meant there was too much of him on show, and it was all good. And totally distracting.

He was stemming the blood flow from his leg wound with his torn trousers and Phoebe stepped in, gently pulling them from his leg so she could check the wound.

The gash was two to three inches long in the muscle of his left calf.

'It's gone in pretty deep,' she told Max. 'But it's missed any major blood vessels.'

'Can you put a couple of stitches in for me?'

'It's too deep for me to fix up here. I'll try to stop the bleeding but you'll need to go to hospital. It must have been a pretty sharp knife to get through two layers of clothing and still do so much damage.'

'He was pretty keen to get away from me. Can't imagine what he was trying to achieve—the house is gutted.'

'If he'd stabbed you a couple of inches lower he probably would have hit your boots and not done any damage at all. But I guess it could be worse.'

Phoebe grabbed the medical kit which was sitting on the stretcher and hunted through it for pressure bandages to hold the wound closed and stem the bleeding. Focussing on the injury, she was able to restore her professional veneer. She wrapped Max's leg, conscious of the firmness of his muscles beneath her fingertips.

'I'll take you around to the ambulance now. Do you need a hand onto the stretcher?'

Max gave her what she could only describe as 'a look'. 'I'll walk. Thanks all the same.'

'You said it hurts to bear weight.'

'It does, but there's no way I'm getting pushed around on a stretcher.'

Phoebe gave him *her* version of 'a look', the one that said *Men!*, and then shrugged her shoulders. 'Have it your way, but you should be keeping your leg elevated.'

'And when we get to the ambulance I'll be a model patient, but there is no way I'm getting wheeled out of here.'

God, he was stubborn. But he was still gorgeous. 'Do you want a hand to get up?' She asked, even though she knew full well what his answer would be.

'I'll be right.' He was cautious, but he made it up off the ground. Pulling his trousers and overalls back on, he tossed his jacket onto the stretcher but he couldn't stop a grimace from escaping as he tried to take a step.

Phoebe pushed the stretcher closer to him.

'Why don't you push one end of this for me? Can your pride handle that?' she teased.

'Thanks, you're a legend.' He was clearly in pain but he still managed a gorgeous smile and, just like that, the world seemed like a better place.

Using the stretcher as a crutch, he walked almost normally. True to his word, he didn't argue once they were at the ambulance but helped her load the stretcher before hopping onto it.

He was even paler under his tan and she knew his leg was hurting. 'Do you want something for the pain?'

'I'll be right.'

'So you keep saying,' she said, not sure whether to be amused, impressed or irritated with how stubborn he was. Did firies, working daily in the role of heroes, break the rule about men being the worst patients?

'What's up?' Steve was beside her.

'Max saved a life and got stabbed for his troubles.'

'You're joking!'

'Unfortunately, she's not, and apparently the wound's too deep to be stitched here. You two are giving me a ride to the hospital.'

Steve glanced at Phoebe who nodded in reply.

'Let's go. Your turn to drive, Phoebes.' He tossed her the keys and climbed in the back beside Max. 'You can tell me all about it on the way back to Hahndorf, mate.'

Phoebe closed the doors and got behind the steering-wheel, half listening to the conversation from the back and half listening to her own internal monologue as she drove.

Who was Max to her?

She was scared to admit he was more than just a new housemate. He stirred up all sorts of feelings, all good. He was the first person in a long time who had been able to do that. Was she ready for it? For one thing, it had been so long she'd forgotten how to respond.

No, not quite true. Her body had no trouble responding to him. A smile, a glance, a kiss from him were all enough to set her pulse racing.

She'd thought all that was finished for her, had convinced herself it was the best way to live her life. She'd made a conscious effort to avoid relationships of any sort, thinking she could protect herself from more heartache. She'd cut herself off from all her friends in her old life. Her girlfriends had tried to keep in touch but she didn't have anything in common with them any more. Not as much anyway, and moving away from Sydney had been a conscious decision, partly because she wanted a fresh start.

Margot was the only friend with whom she still had regular contact. And Phoebe had to admit it was only because Margot had refused to give up on her. Margot still kept ringing even when Phoebe didn't return her calls. She still emailed, still kept Phoebe in the loop with what was happening, letting her know she hadn't been forgotten. Phoebe would have given up a long time ago.

Margot and her husband Glen had been her and Adam's best friends. They'd done most things together and that had been a tough part of watching her marriage fall apart. She had feared losing their friendship but Margot had worked hard at keeping her part of it going, which was more than Phoebe felt she deserved.

Other than her parents, Margot, along with the occasional contact from Adam, was the only survivor from her old life. Even though Phoebe knew she'd never forget what had happened, that didn't mean she wanted to talk about it. She didn't want to be around people, especially not people who knew her history. At least, that's what she'd thought.

Now, thanks to Max, she was reassessing her feelings. Perhaps she didn't want to be alone for ever. Perhaps she didn't want to shut herself off emotionally from everyone. Perhaps there was room in her life for fun and laughter.

And love? What about love?

She tightened her grip around the steering-wheel. She was just getting her head around the possibility of a future that held more than just getting through the day. Contemplating love would be taking it all too far.

Wouldn't it?

'Mum, I'm all grown up. You really can't make me do this,' said Phoebe as she stood in her parents' kitchen, a foil-covered dinner plate in her hand, glaring at Ned who was smirking in the background.

'I promised the poor boy a roast dinner, and the fact he's been hospitalised is all the more reason to take it to him.'

Phoebe opened her mouth, thought better of it and shut it again.

Ned smirked again.

Phoebe re-thought her silence. 'You can come, too. You can cut his meat for him.'

Her mother tutted. Her father had already made himself scarce, having taken one look at the expression on his daughter's face and the hands-on-her-hips stance of his wife. 'How you ended up in a caring profession is beyond me sometimes, Phoebe,' she said as she bustled about covering the remains of their dinner. 'He's your house-mate and a lovely young man.' She stopped bustling and Phoebe could see the light-bulb go on above her head. 'Or is that the problem?' She didn't bother pressing Phoebe, turning instead to the weakest link in the room. 'Ned?'

Ned glanced over his shoulder, clearly wishing he'd followed Phoebe's dad out of the room when he'd had a chance.

'You don't need to say anything, Ned, it's clear as day on your face. Phoebe, that's wonderful news. I won't go on about it, but I can't tell you how happy I am someone's taken your fancy, and someone so lovely to boot. Your father will be thrilled.' She took the plate out of Phoebe's hands, peeled back the foil and added a few more slices of roast lamb to the plate before handing it back to her daughter. 'Max will be needing some pudding, too,' she muttered as she crossed to the fridge and took out the apple pudding she'd only just put away.

Phoebe glared at Ned and made a slicing motion across her throat at which Ned pretended to quiver with fear, only just suppressing laughter, as he mouthed 'Sorry.'

Twenty minutes later, she knew for sure that a blind date couldn't be as excruciating as arriving at a man's hospital bed laden with a twee basket of home-cooked food, when there was no understanding between them at all.

Worse, what if her face gave away she'd been entertaining random—nonsensical!—thoughts about the 'L' word just that afternoon?

Hovering in the doorway of Max's room, Phoebe was a split second away from turning on her heel and depositing the contents of the basket in the bin. But then her mum would ask Max whether he'd enjoyed her cooking. They'd all read much more into her failing to bring it to him than if she just got it over with now.

She knocked and opened the door quickly, pressing the handle as if it would burn her, knowing her courage would fail her if she didn't hurry.

His grin on seeing her was high-wattage. 'Phoebe!'

She deposited the basket of food onto the overway table by his bed and was rewarded with a burst of laughter.

'Is there food in your basket, Little Red Riding Hood? You even dressed the part.'

He grinned again at her discomfort when she realised that, yes, she had indeed sallied forth wearing a red T-shirt. 'There's food—if you behave—but there's no hood, I'm not little and I've never seen a grandmother who looks like you.' Don't mention it, look somewhere else. But, no, her mouth was engaging independently of her brain. 'I'm pretty sure even the wolf wasn't languishing about half-naked.'

Half-naked was not a good thing. Not when she had no clue what to do about feeling this way about him. Feeling she'd love to just climb right in beside him and put her head on his chest and—

'You're right, he was wearing Granny's neck-to-knee nightie, but the closest thing here is hospital gowns, and I don't do gowns. Should I put that on…' he waved a hand at his grubby T-shirt slung over the back of the chair '…to protect your sensibilities?' His face showed his distaste for the idea.

Glancing from Max to the shirt and back again, she searched for something light-hearted to say—witty was too much to hope for—and drew a blank. How could she think with all that perfect chest on show? She should have thought to bring him some clean clothes.

'It's really me, you know, I won't bite,' he said, amused.

'No, I know.' She was so bad at this! 'Here.' She took a step forward, pushing the table closer to Max and whisking the tea-towel off to reveal the contents of the basket. 'It's from Mum,' she added, in case he should think she'd spent the afternoon cooking for him.

'Have you eaten?'

She nodded, distracted by the sight of rippling chest and abdominal muscles as he lifted containers of food from the basket, licking his lips in anticipation of a feast.

'Your mum is an angel.' Peeling back the foil

on the roast dinner, he cut into it. 'Apologies if I ignore you for a moment. A good roast dinner does that to a starving man. Dinner here was hours ago and it wasn't exactly gourmet.' He proceeded to eat his way steadily through the meal, leaving Phoebe feeling she should say something, but all she could think of, as she watched his lips close around the fork, was that he'd kissed her and she wanted more. She just didn't know how to go about it. Focus. Where were basic conversation skills when you needed them?

When he was almost finished, she blurted out, 'How come you didn't tell me you were hurt until after we'd treated that kid? Weren't you in pain?'

He swallowed and looked up from his dinner. Reluctantly? Few men could resist her mum's dinners.

He shrugged. 'I knew I'd live. That kid really did need your attention before me.'

'I realise that, but Steve and I were both there. You didn't have to wait.'

'No harm done.'

'No, you're lying in hospital with thirty stitches in your leg. I know,' she said when he started to query her information. 'I asked the nurses.'

'That's confidential information.' But he didn't seem to mind her knowing in the slightest. 'Jason told you, right?' He paused, scratching his chin, thinking. 'Tell me you didn't bribe him with my dessert.'

For the first time, she relaxed. He was so laid-back it was hard not to fall under his spell. 'Just eat up—you need your strength.'

'For anything in particular?' He raised an eyebrow and a shiver of anticipation ran down her spine.

Memories of Monday night at the pub were occupying her brain, making it impossible for her to answer his question. She could remember exactly how his lips had felt on hers the other night, could remember feeling he could consume her if he wanted to. The sparks she'd felt then were threatening to surface again now and she knew she'd be powerless to resist.

Max dropped the knife and fork onto his plate and didn't take his gaze off her. He leant towards her, ever so slightly, and Phoebe could see the intent in his eyes. She felt her pulse quicken and her breaths become shallow as, with one calm movement, he pushed aside the table and pulled her close. She hesitated for a moment, before letting herself be drawn in to him. No competition, really.

His lips were rougher than when she'd last kissed him and the difference in texture reminded her of how he'd been in danger today, heightening the emotion she felt as they explored each other in their kiss.

She was teetering on the brink of being so absolutely in the moment, this delicious moment, that the past would be forgotten. The allure of his touch, his hold, was too strong and she gave in to the present, leaning in against his chest, reaching her fingers up to his face, the stubble of a day's growth rough under her touch.

A sharp intake of breath from Max brought the hospital room back into focus and the past back into mind.

'Did I hurt you?' She'd wanted to stay in that moment of being nowhere other than in Max's arms. The times he'd held her, kissed her had been almost the only times in these last few years when Joe hadn't been in her mind, at some level, colouring her every thought and feeling.

'I'm fine.' He ruffled her hair. 'I just forgot about my leg for a minute.'

'Sorry.'

'Don't be. It was worth it.'

Phoebe felt herself blushing. This sort of attention was unfamiliar to her now.

'You're stunningly gorgeous, Phoebe, and if a kiss from you means I have to suffer an extra moment of pain, I'm not about to argue.'

She wanted really, really badly to ask him if he meant it. But that would be adolescent, wouldn't it? So, of course, she almost did it, and had to bite her tongue to stop herself.

'Besides, it's not you who caused the injury. If I could get my hands on that kid, I'd—'

'You'd what?' she asked, intrigued, as she shifted away from him until she was sitting halfway along the bed, hoping it was a distancing that had been smooth enough not to be embarrassing.

'I'd have a few choice words for him.'

'No violence?' She teased. 'Tough fireman stuff?'

'I only do my tough fireman stuff if I'm being paid.'

'So if my toaster catches on fire and you're home, you wouldn't come to my rescue?'

'Sure I would.'

She nodded. 'I knew it.'

'I'd dial 000 and get the fire department.'

Laughing, she forgot all about being at a loss over how to behave and picked up the bowl of apple pudding. 'You don't get this until you promise you'd do your tough-guy stuff for me if there's a fire.'

'Is it good?'

She lifted the cover and took a deep breath. 'Mmm. The best.'

'Deal.' He held out a hand for it and she passed it over.

The pudding disappeared in a flash. 'You all but inhaled that, Max. Mum's going to love you.' Then froze at her words—would he think she was implying something?

'Mums always love me.' His grin said it was true and the sparkle in his eyes told her he'd seen her discomfort and knew exactly what she'd been thinking—but was letting her off by not mentioning her *faux pas*. 'I never send a plate back with a crumb on it. You can test my claim when I get out of here if you like. I still have to take you to dinner at the pub. How's Friday night?'

'Will you be up to it?'

He grinned again and Phoebe was blushing

before he even said anything. 'It's just dinner, I'm sure I can handle that. And I promise to resist you if you want to tear my clothes off.' She felt her blush deepen. 'Patience is one of my virtues.'

She laughed and rolled her eyes. 'I'm sure you have many virtues.'

'More than our friendly neighbourhood moron, at any rate. According to the guys, that idiot had a drug lab in the house. He's just lucky the explosion didn't kill someone.' He packed the plate, bowl and cutlery back into the basket, folding the tea-towel expertly on top. Her mum *would* love him. 'As it is, he's destroyed four houses.'

'Do you know what he wanted when he went back in?'

He shrugged. 'Probably money.'

'A big sum?'

'The investigation will take some time, but the guys guess he could have had hundreds of thousands of dollars go up in smoke.'

'Hence making it worth his while to go into a burning building.'

'It makes my blood boil, people who think about themselves and no one else. All that focus on money, going hard at it to make their fortune and not caring who gets hurt along the way. It's the disease of the modern world.'

'Crime is everywhere?'

He shook his head. 'Not just illicit money. The obsession with money is rampant in our society, everything is sacrificed at its altar, nothing's sacred any more. Relationships are defined by it, self-worth centres on it and people worship it like it's a god. Greed. Greed and selfishness.'

The joy that had blossomed in her heart was extinguished bit by bit with each new word Max spoke. 'Money is sort of a necessary evil, Max. The bills have to be paid. People have to live.'

'They don't have to live by trampling over other people to get more money, they don't have to live by wanting more than they need. None of us need half of what we have, yet most of the world seems to think they don't just want more, they actually need it. And the things that are really important are forgotten in the first place.'

'You're not just talking about today, are you?'

He shrugged, a lopsided smile lighting up his face again. He'd already dropped his passionate stance and was half laughing at his outburst. 'I'm talking about my personal bug bear. The stupidity of the crazy pursuit of money is something close to my heart.'

'I can see.' She picked at the white cotton blanket under her fingertips. 'I'd better let you get some rest. You'll be home tomorrow?'

'Ned's picking me up first thing.' There was a quizzical look on his face but she stood up before he could ask her any questions, fussing with the basket to avoid having to meet his eyes. 'Are you home tomorrow night?' he continued. 'Your healing touch might be required.'

'I'll see you then.' She deliberately didn't pick up on his last comment, just leant in to drop a kiss on his lips, resisting the urge to linger. He wouldn't be looking at her like she was lovely if he knew everything there was to know about her, so she shouldn't be getting used to his touch, or the way his lips felt.

She headed for the door, and turned to wave, a forced smile in place. As she stepped in the hall, out of his view, he called out, 'I feel better already, you make a great doctor.'

She froze at the words—did he know? No, her parents wouldn't have told him. Ned? She shook her head. No, he wouldn't sell her out. It had been a chance remark, that was all.

She whispered, 'I *did* make a great doctor.' Blinking back the tears that were burning her eyes, she strode down the corridor, basket clenched in her white-knuckled fingers.

She should have known better than to think she'd get another shot at life. She knew she didn't deserve it, she didn't deserve more than this half-life she was living, and she'd tempted the gods by daring to dream. Fate had teased her with a glimpse of how things could have been, before coldly slamming shut the door to that alternate future. 'I did make a great doctor,' she repeated to herself. 'Just not for my own child.'

CHAPTER SEVEN

'MRS WILSON, it pains me to say it...' Max swivelled in his chair positioned at Phoebe's parents' computer desk '...but I can't possibly eat another piece of cake or take another bite of slice.'

'Call me Nina,' said Phoebe's mum.

At the same time Phoebe's dad said, 'What about me?' as he eyed off the plate of home-baked offerings his wife was holding.

She slapped her husband's hand away good-naturedly. 'You've driven me mad since you've retired, but that's no reason to send you to an early grave with heart disease.' She held the plate out of reach and said to Max, 'David has high cholesterol and is on a strict diet. It's hard on him because he can't eat what he wants and me because I can't cook what I want. So I'm very glad to have Ned and now you to fatten up instead.'

'What about fattening Phoebe up? There's not much of her.'

'I do my best but nothing sticks to her ribs since…' She trailed off, the anxious glance she gave her husband a give-away that she'd been about to breach an off-limits topic. David took advantage of his wife's moment of distraction, helping himself to the largest piece of slice as the plate was lowered within reach.

'Nothing sticks to her ribs since she's started running,' Nina amended with a note of relief, which Max was sure was because she'd hit on a believable alternate answer. 'She runs so far and so fast it's a surprise there's anything left of her.'

He'd thought there was something more going on in Phoebe's life than she'd divulged to him. She seemed vulnerable and he'd noticed a haunted look in her eyes at times, most recently last night when he'd spoken about money and she'd all but bolted for the door. If he played his hand right, maybe he'd find some answers now.

'She hasn't always been a runner?'

Nina wasn't being caught out that easily. She'd given herself a scare and was playing it safe now. She'd caught David with his mouth full and was tut-tutting at him. He was sure she was using it as chance to end the conversation and think about her answer.

'She was always athletic, and these last few years she's really taken a shine to running. She's a natural, like her dad.'

'Like I was before I got old and blurry 'round the edges.' David beamed. 'Now all I'm good for is sedate activities befitting the elderly and infirm. Like working out how this damn-fool computer works.'

'I'll leave you boys to it,' said Nina, bearing her plate from the room with her, leaving David sighing longingly after it. Max concentrated on the screen, a job he could do while his brain was really scrolling through the hints that there was a secret in Phoebe's past. Surely it had to be something more than a failed marriage.

'Almost there. Your system was chock-a-block with rubbish and you had some interesting settings on your virus programme that was slowing it down.' He showed David how to update his virus search and reminded him to scan for cookies, something it was clear he'd forgotten to do, if he'd ever known.

But what he was really thinking was how he was going to find out about Phoebe. She'd been running for a few years. And there had been some event that had been so traumatic she hadn't kept weight on since. Had that been before or after she'd started running? Was that why she started running? And the haunted look in her eyes—was that due to memories she needed to run from?

He didn't like secrets.

He didn't like anyone deceiving him.

He did like Phoebe.

But if Phoebe was hiding a secret from him, was she the woman he'd started to think she was?

'He's what?' Phoebe stopped in mid-stretch when she heard Ned's reply to her question about Max's whereabouts. 'I would've cleared up their computer if they'd asked me. Mum will ask him to move in next.' She resumed a thigh stretch and tried to clear the scowl from her face. Her parents were going to make this much, much harder than it needed to be.

'What's the issue? He's housebound for a couple of days, your dad needed some help, Max

offered when your mum brought some food over.'
Ned was curious. 'You're interested, he's interested, but you're blowing hot and cold. I know he's the first guy you've fancied since you spilt with Adam and you're nervous, but I can tell there's more to it. What's going on?'

She ignored his question. 'Are you going to warm up and come with me?'

'Nope, I worked out at the station this morning—that's enough for any self-respecting male. Besides, I can't keep up with you, you know that. Stop changing the subject and tell me what the problem is.'

'I chose you for my best friend because you didn't ask lots of questions,' Phoebe said, concentrating on her balance, her foot crossed over one knee as she took up a yoga stretch.

'Speaking of best friends, Margot rang. She wants to know if you've booked your flight to Sydney for her birthday.'

'Not yet.'

'She seems to think you'll be going. Will you?'

'I guess,' she said, sounding less than enthusiastic. Margot was turning thirty and Phoebe had no good reason not to help her celebrate. Except it would be the first big party she'd been to in three years. She still wasn't sure she could handle it. Or even if she was ready to try.

'I know you're nervous. Would you like me to come with you?' Phoebe glanced up at Ned and he grinned as he clarified his offer. 'There's always a shortage of single, straight guys at those Sydney parties. I'd be doing everyone a favour.'

'Honestly, Ned, you are hopeless.' She started laughing, nearly losing her balance, and had to grab the doorframe for support. 'So you'd walk me into the party and then abandon me the minute we got there to chase after all the young single girls?'

He shook his head. 'I'd hang around with you for a bit. You can introduce me to your girlfriends.'

'Thanks but, no, thanks.'

'Why don't you ask Max to go with you, then?'

It was her turn to shake her head. 'I don't think that's a good idea.'

'Why not?'

'Let's just say we have some differences of opinion.'

'That explanation's about as clear as mud.'

'He can't stand anything to do with money

and, from what I can gather, anyone who has monetary goals.'

'He said that?' She nodded and Ned elaborated. 'His parents have always been on at him to pursue a high-paying career. You know he studied engineering?' She nodded again. 'And he was always dead set on doing the opposite. Since he came back from Canada, he's even more set on keeping his music alive in the face of any opposition and refusing to cave in and do a job just for the prestige or the money.'

'So what would he think of me?'

'That you're over-thinking this particular situation?'

She gave him 'the look', as Ned called it, and squatted down to retie her laces tightly. 'What would he think of the old me?'

'The one who was doing her best to juggle ten balls with only two hands and precious few juggling skills?'

She looked up from her position on the floor. 'The me who didn't know her child was critically ill because she was so busy working to try and meet the mortgage payments.' She stood and shook her limbs out for a moment, all ready to run.

'He'd think you'd done your best, Phoebe.'

Phoebe shook his words off like water. 'Thanks, Ned, but it won't help. You asked me what was going on. That's what's going on and there's no point thinking I can do anything about it.' She was at the door, bouncing up and down on the balls of her feet, too uptight to stand still. She needed a hard, fast run to work out her agitation. 'I'll see you in a bit.'

Max arrived back at the cottage to see Phoebe disappearing at speed over a distant hilltop. He watched her until she disappeared from view then followed the sound of wood-chopping out to the shed where he found Ned splitting logs for the Wilsons. Ned would have the answers.

He got straight to the point. 'There's some whopping great secret in her past, Ned, and she runs like she's terrified it's going to catch her any second.' Ned glanced at him between logs but stayed silent. Was he going to make him work for his information? 'Her mum's terrified she'll give something away and you protect her like she's your defenceless little sister. And that's the real clincher. That's how I *know* there's something

I'm not being told, because there's no way under ordinary circumstances you wouldn't be after her. What's the deal?'

Ned pulled the axe from the log, raised it and brought it down with a crash, splitting the log in two, before he answered. 'You'll have to talk to her.'

'So there is something?'

He shrugged. 'I don't think so. I mean, yes, something happened and she thinks it'll…' He tailed off then tried again. 'But I don't see why it should…' He stopped, flustered. 'Listen, mate, I don't want to get caught in the middle. It's not for me to tell you. You have to ask her. But go easy, OK? It wasn't nice and she hasn't got over it.'

'What wasn't nice? I know she was married, is it that? A nasty break-up and she's scared of getting hurt again? We've all been there.'

'No, mate, I don't think we've all been where Phoebe's been. But are you saying that, if that's all it was, you'd be interested?' He'd put his axe down on the chopping block and fixed Max with a hard stare. 'You're getting serious about her? There's no point asking her to explain anything if you're not.'

'Because?'

'Because she would only confide in you if she had some pretty powerful feelings for you. If you cut and run after that, it'll just make her believe all the more that she's a bad person.'

Max ground his teeth in frustration. 'I wish you'd just tell me what this is all about. I can't get serious if I think she's hiding something from me. I've been there, done that. How am I meant to know how I feel about her when I know there's some big secret lurking in her past? Yet you say I can't ask her until I know how I feel. It's a no-win situation.'

Ned shrugged. 'I can't help you, mate. The only advice I have is what I've already said—let it go now if you're not serious about her. It's not fair to her.' He picked up his axe, effectively closing the conversation.

Max turned on his heel and retreated to the house. He'd have loved to have taken his frustrations out on that wood, but he knew his calf wouldn't stand up to swinging an axe any time soon. He wouldn't even be back on office duties for another day.

He opened the back door and walked past the

kitchen, tossing his jacket onto a chair, and into the little library. Phoebe's French books were lying on the window-seat and from there he could just see her figure as she ran along the far ridge of a hill. Even at this distance he could see she was still running at speed.

She was definitely running from something.

And, according to Ned, he couldn't know exactly what that something was unless he could answer one question himself: did he want to catch her?

She was so tired of running, she thought as she stopped at the Shady Pool to do her warm-down stretches. She'd run every day this week, and for longer than usual. There was no denying Max was the reason. Or, to be more specific, her desire to avoid Max was the reason.

She'd chosen to work in a male-dominated pro-fession because men, as a rule, didn't cross-examine anyone and so far it had worked for her. She didn't want to answer questions about herself or her life. Her colleagues respected that. They treated her as one of them. They didn't criticise or try and make her what she wasn't. They let her be.

Max wasn't treating her any differently but she

knew there were questions he wanted to ask her, and the prospect frightened her. And it was that prospect she wanted to avoid, not Max himself. If she knew her past wouldn't come up, she'd like nothing more than to see Max. But he had questions, she'd sensed it. If she answered them, he'd judge her. Who wouldn't? Especially when he was so determined that money wouldn't be a priority in his life.

Max had breached her defences. He'd had made her vulnerable.

Now it was easier just to avoid him, and running was helping do just that.

Today, though, time had run out. This morning they were doing the kindergarten visit. And tonight they'd planned dinner.

Only a few days ago she'd been looking forward to today. Now she felt torn between a physical, aching need to see him and anxiety over his reaction if—when!—he found out about everything there was to know.

'Can I put your siren on?'

'Daniel says he's driven an ambliance before. He's four. Can I try?'

'My brother says you don't got no windows 'cos you only take dead people.'

The kindergarten director was doing her best to keep the order but the group of twenty children sitting cross-legged on the mat was squirming with excitement. They looked like a posse of lemmings and one was bound to break free at any second.

Phoebe fielded the questions as best she could while Steve hovered behind her, turning a noticeable shade of grey. 'I've got head spins,' he whispered in her ear when he had a chance. 'There's so many of them and they're so…so… wriggly.'

'When's the firemen coming?' piped up a little girl, for whom the only polite adjective Phoebe could come up with was 'over-active'.

'Ah, we get to the main event.' Phoebe addressed the teachers. 'That's why we come first. Once the fire engine arrives, it's all over for us.'

'That's how it is for us the minute anyone new walks through the door!' responded one of the teachers.

A brief 'whoop' of a siren heralded the arrival of the fire engine, sending the children into fits of delighted excitement. Phoebe stood back, amused, watching the staff try and restore order.

'They could eat us alive!' muttered Steve as he bolted for the door.

'Funny, that's exactly what I feel is about to happen.' If only she was talking about the children. But it was the thought of seeing Max that was reducing her to a state of nervous tension. Largely because she'd so successfully managed to avoid him since his discharge.

But avoiding him indefinitely wasn't going to happen, so she followed the line of giggling four-year-olds outside the kindergarten building. The fire engine was parked out the front behind the ambulance. Ned, Cookie and Nifty were standing in front of it, ready to talk to the children. Where was Max? Ned shifted slightly and she saw Max, sitting on the step of the truck. Was his calf too sore to take his weight?

Once the children were settled on the small grassy hill in the park beside the kindergarten building, Max stood and began the session, so it seemed he was managing OK on his leg. Phoebe stood with Steve behind the children, listening and watching as Max talked to the class about fire safety.

He was lovely with them. Not forced. Not condescending, just simply lovely. He had them all in fits of laughter at the end of the short talk when he got Ned to demonstrate how to stop, drop, cover and roll then got them all to practise it themselves.

Phoebe stood quietly, surreptitiously watching Max. Even though she'd been trying to avoid him, now he was here she couldn't stop herself from watching him. She was drawn to his natural charisma. He was roaring with laughter at the antics of some of the more confident children, who were taking great delight in over-dramatising the stop, drop and cover before rolling down the small hill.

Max seemed his normal self whereas she was a mass of confusion. She wondered if he even realised she'd been avoiding him or whether he knew but wasn't bothered about it. Had he remembered they'd planned dinner at the pub tonight? She couldn't go, could she? But how was she going to get out if it?

There he was, having a grand time with the rowdier children, while she stood with the few children who were hanging back. She wanted to be able to join him, wanted to be free to have dinner with him without feeling churned up with nerves, but instead she was here, standing with the same small group of children who had hung back when she and Steve had shown them the ambulance and their equipment. They were the more tentative ones, not as confident but every bit as interested. Did they get overlooked, these less pushy little people? Did life rush by them, leaving them behind? Or did they find their place somewhere or another in the huge world?

This whole morning was an uncomfortable analogy for her life. She was being left behind while the rest of the world raced past her. A lack of sleep wasn't helping, sure, but she felt like these children who were standing next to her, standing on the rim, looking at what she really wanted and knowing she'd never have it. The other children were lining up now, getting ready to file through the fire engine. She could see the more tentative ones glancing that way, anxiety on their faces, worried they'd miss out on the chance to take a look.

As she watched, she felt a soft little hand sneak its way into her palm and she closed her fingers tight around it. She didn't have to look to know who it was—she even knew his name. It was

Alex, the little boy who, from the moment she and Steve had arrived, had watched them like they were superheroes, adoration plain in his expressive dark eyes. He'd grabbed her heart the first moment she'd seen him. He had Joe's colouring. At least, the colouring she imagined Joe would have kept.

But it was Alex, not Joe. Swallowing, focussing, she switched off the part of her heart that would never heal. Never heal and never forget.

Squatting down, she looked into Alex's eyes. 'You like fire engines and ambulances a fair bit, hey, Alex?'

'Lots and lots,' was his whispered reply. He was looking back and forth between her and the fire engine. Her and nirvana. That was how Max had looked at her! But he didn't know the truth and she wasn't sticking around to find out how he looked at her once he *did* know.

'Would you like to see the fire engine?' The offer was made as casually as she could. She'd seen him watching the stream of children file through the rear of the truck, all emerging with grins and shining eyes.

His eyes grew larger, if that were possible, and

his gaze didn't leave hers as he nodded solemnly. 'Will you take me?'

'Absolutely. I know some people who know some people.' She led him over, trying not to think about how Joe's hand would have felt just like this in hers, walking hand in hand. He'd even have been Alex's age. Almost.

But now he was six months old for ever.

She bit back tears and suppressed a cry of raw pain that surprised her with its intensity. The pain would never leave, she'd never be the same person she'd been before Joe, but nowadays it was usually a dull ache, not this brutal, stabbing pain which could take her breath away. Tightening her fingers ever so gently around Alex's, she looked down at him while he chatted shyly with her. Having the idea of Max dangled in front of her then blown apart had touched a nerve she hadn't known was so exposed.

'We should be selling these,' Cookie said to Max. 'We'd make a small fortune just driving around to kindergartens in our spare time and running a fire-hat stall from the back of the truck.'

They were handing out red plastic fire hats to

each of the children as they climbed down from the fire engine, little hands held up, little bodies bouncing with eagerness. Over the top of the sea of little heads Max looked up and saw Phoebe watching him, her expression thoughtful.

Ned's warning flashed through his mind. Ned had him thoroughly mixed-up, torn between what he wanted to do with Phoebe, which was take their relationship one step on from dinner and kisses, and what was apparently the noble thing to do, which was to leave her alone unless he was sure he was serious.

Looking her way again, he met her gaze. Flicking his glance to her mouth, a smile came to his own. Noble be hanged. They were adults. Ned wasn't her father, and surely he and Phoebe could just have a conversation and sort things out? They were having dinner tonight. There'd be no interruptions and he'd get this confusion resolved.

He handed out another plastic helmet and watched as that child took off, joining his mates who were all running around the grass, hats on heads, pretending to hose down the playground equipment and drive imaginary fire trucks, screeching out their version of blaring sirens.

'Max.'

He turned back to the truck. 'Hi, there.' Phoebe was standing in front of him, holding a little boy tight by the hand, and he didn't know which of them looked more nervous, adult or child.

Her smile, when it came, was tentative. 'Max, this is Alex. He'd like to see inside the fire engine.'

'G'day, mate.' Max bent down to the little boy's level, conscious of making a good impression with the children, with Phoebe. It shouldn't matter in the slightest, especially in the circumstances. But it did. 'I think we can arrange that.' Phoebe let go of Alex's hand and Max lifted him into the front seat of the appliance. The other children had filed through across the back seats but Max had something more special in mind for Alex.

'Would you like to put the siren on?'

Alex didn't take his eyes off Max and simply nodded, his face shining.

As a general rule only the fire crew got to put the siren on, very briefly, as they arrived and departed from a PR visit. It was only on a very rare occasion that they let a child do it. Let one and they'd all want to was a lesson he'd learned long ago. But he sensed this shy little boy would remember this moment for a long time and he wanted to be the one who could make a difference. Or did he think he'd score brownie points with Phoebe? Points he sensed he might need?

'We'll check with your teacher but we won't tell the other children yet. Deal?'

Alex nodded again, his cheeks flushed pink. He waited, silently, as Max spoke to the director then watched, his little face solemn with concentration, as Max explained about the switches to turn on the lights and siren.

The director called the other children back to the fire engine to thank the team as Alex waited, unnoticed, in the cabin with Max.

'Are you ready?' Max asked him.

'Yes.' It was the first time he'd spoken to Max.

'OK, champ. Time for the siren.'

Alex didn't need to be asked twice—he knew exactly which button was the one and he pressed it. Nineteen pairs of hands covered little ears as Alex turned the siren on for a blissful—for him, Max wasn't sure of the neighbours—five seconds.

'Turn it off now,' said Max, and Alex did. Max grimaced as he looked out the window and now saw nineteen children rioting to have a go with the siren, the director making short work of restoring order and Phoebe looking at him, shaking her head and laughing.

'That was awesome,' Alex said, his face upturned to Max's.

Max laughed. 'Awesome? Where did you learn that word?'

'My babysitter. Everyone's going to wish they'd done the siren.'

Max was about to ruffle his hair then stopped himself. He'd hated that as a kid. He held up a hand instead, saying, 'Give me some skin, man.'

Alex high-fived him and Max helped him down from the cabin. Phoebe was there to swing Alex down the last step. She was saying goodbye to Alex and he spontaneously stepped into her arms to give her a hug. She'd closed her eyes and Max could've sworn she was somewhere else in her mind, not here. Sworn she was holding someone else.

Was that the glimmer of tears in her now opened eyes as she whispered in Alex's ear? He giggled and ran off to join the line of children snaking their way back into the kindergarten, chaos erupting again as they all tried to gather around him as the teachers tried their best to keep everyone moving.

'Glad that's their job, not mine,' said Cookie.

Phoebe sniffed.

'I'm done over,' said Steve.

Phoebe wiped her eyes with the back of her hand.

'We'd better be off. I need a coffee,' said Cookie.

Phoebe was silent, looking off into the direction of the children, who had now disappeared from view.

'I need lunch,' said Steve.

'What about you, Phoebe?' Max was intrigued. Something had happened just now and he didn't have a clue what it was. Only that he wanted to know. 'What do you need?'

'A swim.' She was decisive. She was smiling. And she wasn't telling the truth. There was something else she needed. The desire was plain in her eyes. 'But that will have to wait until after work.'

'And after your swim, are you still up for dinner?'

'Dinner?'

'The meal that comes a few hours after lunch,' he said, liking the way her cheeks coloured just a little with his teasing. He liked it in spite of the reservations that had bugged him every moment since his conversation with Ned had confirmed there was something he didn't know about Phoebe. Something he needed to know.

She hesitated. Uncertainty flickered in her blue eyes, and he knew there were thoughts aplenty racing through that mind of hers. Cataloguing all the reasons she didn't want to spend more time with him? He'd been talking himself out of wanting things to progress further with her but hadn't stopped to think she might be doing the same. Was that why their paths hadn't crossed since Wednesday? Because she'd had a change of heart and had been avoiding *him*?

He had a sudden sense she might cancel their date. He wasn't prepared to let that happen. There was something important he needed to know, he was certain of that. Curiosity would kill him. Working with her, sharing a house with her while leaving this attraction between them unresolved would kill him. He couldn't do it. He had to have some answers.

She nodded, slowly, considering. 'OK. I suppose we'd better do it—' She broke off, embarrassed. 'That came out the wrong way. There are some things I need to tell you, though, and I guess I'm not looking forward to it.'

'You don't think we'll still be able to enjoy dinner?'

She looked him straight in the eye. 'Actually, I'm afraid I'll enjoy dinner but you'll wish you were anywhere else but there.' The simplicity and openness of her confession surprised him and, strangely, it looked like it startled her.

'Shall we risk it?'

She smiled again but her smile didn't reach her eyes and her shoulders were rigid with stored tension.

'Yes,' she said, then turned on her heel and strode to the waiting ambulance.

Leaving him with precisely no idea, absolutely none at all, what was going on in her head. And more than a little concerned that Ned might be right and he'd end the night wishing he hadn't found out.

Phoebe was heading up the path towards the house as Max got home. She was in her bathers, her towel slung over her shoulder, obviously coming back from the waterhole after her swim. He would have loved to have joined her, the cool water would be a refreshing tonic at the end of the day, but he still had stitches in his leg. Plus, he hadn't been invited.

She hadn't seen him yet and he stood, keys dangling from his hand. He needed to sit down, to ease the dull throb that was building in his leg, but he wanted to wait for her.

Judging by the bright glow in her cheeks and the fact her breath was coming hard and fast, she'd had a vigorous swim, but her strides were still long and she didn't look exhausted. And judging by the way the glow in her cheeks deepened when she saw him, the feelings he was having for her were mutual. Or was she just anxious about whatever it was she had to tell him?

'Hey, there,' he said.

'Hi. Is your leg bothering you?' She'd taken one look at him and seen he was favouring his left leg. 'Let's go in. I'll check it out if you like.'

He really shouldn't tempt himself with personal contact but... 'Thanks.' The pain *was* getting worse. 'A whole day on it has taken its toll.'

The silence that fell between them as they went inside could have been uncomfortable but the mutual heightened awareness he could feel between them didn't leave much room for anything else.

He sat on the window-seat in the library. The

silence stretched on. He was aware of her long legs, lightly tanned and toned as she sat beside him. His gaze flicked over her smooth skin and followed the length of her limbs up to where her skin disappeared beneath the Lycra of her swimsuit. Her waist was trim but the fabric struggled to contain her breasts. The halterneck cut of her bathers pushed her breasts together and the two perfect spheres threatened to spill over as she moved. She shifted on the seat, pulling her towel into her lap, hiding behind its flimsy protection.

'You'll have to take your jeans off.' Her voice was husky. Their eyes met and he noticed hers were almost an exact match to the blue of her bathers. The blush that had been fading in her cheeks reappeared and she continued, flustered, 'If you want me to look at your wound.'

He didn't speak, just stood, kicked off his shoes and undid the buttons of his jeans, keeping his gaze fixed on hers as he pushed his jeans past his hips until he was standing before her in his underwear.

Phoebe was the first to break eye contact. He saw her swallow as she dropped her gaze to his injured calf.

'Sit down and I'll take the bandage off.'

Max did as he was told, lifting his left leg up onto the window-seat, putting his foot close to Phoebe's lap. Her fingers trembled as she unwrapped the bandage.

'The area around the stitches is a little red but nothing out of the ordinary.' Her fingers were cool on his skin as she checked the wound. 'You're taking your antibiotics?'

'Of course.'

'Then the discomfort is most likely because you've overused your leg today. But if it gets worse, you should go back to your doctor.' She looked back at him, her hand still resting on his leg, and he was so conscious of her touch he couldn't reply. 'I'll rebandage it for you.' She spoke in a whisper and he knew then she was as affected as he was by their proximity, their near nakedness.

His gaze dropped to her mouth. Her lips were pink, soft, moist, inviting.

Phoebe was rolling the bandage ready to reapply it. She worked quickly. Was she uncomfortable, did she want to get this over with? She finished rolling and began to wind the bandage around his calf, talking as she worked.

'We can cancel dinner.'

'So you keep saying.'

'I mean, if you're tired.' She paused, wrapping the bandage over itself and fixing the end. 'If your leg's tired.'

'I'm fine.' He stood, trying to clear his mind of the images their state of undress was promoting. He pulled his jeans on, his hips only inches from her face.

Phoebe sprang to her feet but that only served to bring her closer to him. His hand brushed her hip as he buttoned his jeans and the physical contact made her gasp, her gaze flying straight to his. Her eyes were enormous, her pupils dark in contrast to the blue of her irises.

He leant forwards, a centimetre or two at the most, so slightly he wasn't aware he'd moved until he felt her breast brush against his chest. He dipped his head and put one hand on her hip. She tilted her head up, their lips inches apart. He pulled her closer. She didn't resist. Didn't protest.

He whispered her name and then he bent his head another inch and claimed her mouth with his.

Her lips were cool and soft. She tasted incredible. He slid his hand off her hip and further up her back, holding her tight against his body.

She moaned softly and he deepened the kiss. Her lips opened under his touch, parting slightly to let his tongue in. His fingers slipped underneath the straps of her bathers but before he could explore any further she pulled away.

'Max. Wait.' She caught his hand against her right shoulder. 'I can't do this.'

'I beg to differ. You're doing it perfectly.' He bent his head, intending to kiss her again.

She held up her hands, blocking him. 'Don't.'

He stopped. 'Don't what?'

'Don't kiss me again.'

'Why not?'

'I can't.'

'*You can't* is not a reason.' He took hold of her hands, capturing them in his and holding them to his chest, relishing the feel of her skin, the warmth of her fingers wrapped in his. 'You're scared to explore this attraction between us. You've been avoiding me since I was discharged from hospital. I have no intention of hurting you but I also have no intention of playing guessing games.'

'I don't mean to run hot and cold.' She took a deep breath. 'But I'm confused.'

'I need to know where I stand, Phoebe. I've been caught before.'

'What do you mean, caught?'

'You know I was involved with a woman in Canada, Lisbette, the one who taught me to speak French?' She nodded. 'We lived together, she had a son, Jacques. I supported us as a family, looked after Jacques more than she did. It's fair to say I was smitten with her.' His dry laugh gave a wry slant to his words. 'I knew she was selfish, immature even, but she was sufficiently charming to get away with it. Plus, I was young and inexperienced and I'd never met anyone like her. I fell hard.' He grimaced, remembering just how quickly he'd been drawn into her life.

'What happened?'

'I found out after more than a year she'd been having an affair with her ex all that time. I was a meal ticket, a convenient source of babysitting, both of which left her free to be with the man she wanted. And there I was, prize chump, thinking she was as besotted with me as I was with her. In retrospect, it all seems so bloody obvious: the stories that didn't add up; myriad little signs something was off. But I didn't see it. I still don't know if I just didn't want to see or whether it's something I wouldn't see again.'

From the look on her face, she didn't feel sorry for him, which was a good sign. The victim role was not for him. He was pretty sure her expression was one of incredulity.

When she spoke, her voice was quiet. 'She hurt you a great deal.'

He grunted in agreement.

'You said you've been caught before, implying you think it might happen again. Do you think I might turn out like her? That I might do something like that and you wouldn't know?'

'You're nothing like her.' Which was true, but there was also a niggle of doubt. Was it really ever safe to trust anyone? And if he did, had he really learnt enough from his time with Lisbette to know if something was wrong? 'You're much more charming,' he said, and this time his words matched the tone of his voice, easing the tension in the room a little. 'And a lot more grown-up.' No, Phoebe was nothing like Lisbette, and if they were open about everything, there was no room for dangerous lies. 'Actually, you're nothing like anyone else I've ever met.'

'That's a good thing, right?'

'Absolutely. You seem more real somehow. There's a connection between us, and I haven't felt that with anyone before, clearly, since I haven't been close to being involved with anyone since Canada. And the connection between us is not the same as it was with Lisbette. That was the besotted blindness of youth.'

'Then if you feel I'm so different, that *we're* so different, what did you mean when you said you'd been caught before?'

'What I meant was, secrets are poison. If there's something you're worried about, something you think could affect you and me, I need to know.' He couldn't spell it out any more clearly. If she was different to Lisbette, she'd confide in him. That's what he needed before he could risk getting involved. 'And there is something you haven't told me.'

'Yes.' Her voice was so soft he only just heard her.

'To do with your marriage?' She nodded, then shrugged, like she wasn't sure, so he asked the question that seemed the obvious one. 'Is it really over?'

She sat down again on the window-seat,

pulling him down beside her. Her towel was lying, forgotten, on the floor but she pulled a cushion into her lap and fiddled with the silky tassel tied at one corner.

'Technically, I'm married, but not for long. That's not what this is about.' She'd found a loose piece of cotton protruding from the cushion's stitching and she was worrying at it with slender fingers, seeming unaware of her fidgeting. 'My husband and I had a son. Joe.'

Ah, the connection with Alex this morning at the kindergarten made more sense. But past tense? Where was he now?

He waited, giving her space to talk.

'And the reason our marriage fell apart was because…because Joe got sick.' Phoebe paused. Max stayed quiet, sensing she needed time. 'He died.'

The tears he'd seen that morning, the doubts he'd sensed in her, the pulling away from him fell into place.

And then, quietly, like she was confessing a crime for which she'd already been sentenced, she added, 'And it was my fault.'

CHAPTER EIGHT

HER first announcement had caused Max no surprises. Her second was met with sympathy. But
at her third she saw shock. He did his best to
cover it with a mask of understanding and compassion but she'd seen the doubt that had been his
automatic reaction.

'Phoebe, I'm so sorry, as useless as that is to
say.' She nodded her acceptance of his words.
'When did he die?'

'Three years ago.'

'How?'

So she told him.

Told him how in a past life she'd been studying
to be a paediatrician—there were questions he
wanted to ask about that, she knew, but he stayed
quiet, letting her talk. She'd married Adam, her
boyfriend from uni, a fellow doctor, and there'd

been no end to their plans. They'd been so excited about the life they were about to start after all the years of studying and making do. They had bought their dream house and had known nothing would stop them from achieving their goals. Then her husband had quit his specialty, having regretted his choice, and changed to the physicians programme, with a killer study schedule and exam requirements and bad pay. They had done their sums and decided they could manage the mortgage on her salary for the time being.

They'd had no plans to have a baby. Their focus had been on working hard to get themselves set up, maybe travel for a while. Children hadn't been in their life plan for at least another five years, maybe longer now Adam had been studying again. They'd still had years ahead of them before they thought about children.

She told him how she'd only just started a great job at the Royal Children's Hospital in Sydney, a coveted job, one she wouldn't get again in a hurry. How there was no way they could meet the mortgage if she wasn't working.

Told him how all the pressures and changed expectations had made it seem the only choice was to opt for a nanny and child care, go back to work full time within ten weeks of the birth, hold on for the ride and hope for the best.

'And what happened?'

'We got into a rhythm, a routine, and mostly it worked. I was overworked, overtired, riddled with guilt all the time, because even when I was with Joe, I'd just keep thinking how it wasn't enough, I should've been with him all the time. But we managed, because we had to. Then, when he was six months old, Joe got a cold, a slight temperature—nothing major, or so we thought. Adam and I went to work and left Joe with the nanny. She called us later but got hold of Adam first. She said Joe seemed worse, he was a bit fretful and had vomited. Adam told her to take him to an all-night clinic. The doctors there sent them home again.

'I'd taken a double shift to cover a flu outbreak among staff at the hospital and the first I knew of any of it was when Adam brought Joe in to the Children's, where I was working. And by that time it was too late.'

He leant towards her as though to pull her in against him, comfort her, but she wasn't having any of it. She'd seen the doubts cloud his eyes when she'd spoken of going straight back to work. He'd judged her. And why wouldn't he? She deserved to be judged, deserved to have him think the worst of her. It was all true.

'What happened?'

She stilled. She hadn't ever described what had happened. She'd never wanted to put into words how it had felt, holding her son's lifeless body, feeling his limp little fingers which would never clutch hers again, looking at his beautiful face, so peaceful as he'd lain in her arms. How it had felt as his skin had grown cold as she'd held him to her heart and how she'd felt, watching him, knowing he'd never smile at her again, knowing she'd never hear him call her name.

She didn't have the words now. She stuck to the facts and left the emotion, the utter, inde-scribable horror of having her baby die in her arms, well alone.

'He had meningococcal meningitis. By the time he was brought in, it had progressed too far, too quickly.' Why was she telling him this much when she never spoke about it and she was sure he'd already judged her? All she felt was numb—

maybe that explained it. It didn't matter how much he knew, the outcome was already determined and he'd pull away from her.

'If I'd been home, I would have known something was wrong. I was a paediatrician but more importantly I was his mother. But I wasn't home, I was at work, making money looking after other people's children. So by the time Joe was brought in, it was too late. There was nothing that could be done.'

Not that she'd accepted that. She'd gone crazy with fear and anything and everything possible *had* been done, but in the end Joe had never had a chance.

'He ended up in ICU, on life support, as his body shut down. There was nothing anyone could do. They couldn't save my baby.' She took a deep breath, fighting for control. 'I should have been there for him. I was his mother. But I wasn't there and now he's gone.'

'Phoebe.' Max's voice was soft. In it she heard caring and she couldn't detect judgment. But she knew she had to bear the responsibility for Joe's death for the rest of her days so she also knew the judgement was there somewhere. Besides, she'd seen it in his eyes when she'd first told him. He'd just had ten or so minutes to get his game face on.

'Phoebe,' he said again, and she resisted the invitation in his voice to look at him, let him comfort her. The comfort would be short-lived when the judgement surfaced again, as it would, so she didn't want to know what it felt like. 'I can't imagine what it's like to lose a child, so I won't pretend I can. But I do know it's normal for someone who loses a child to blame themselves. I've seen it enough times over the years in my job to know that. And I know you must be terrified of letting someone close again.' He leant forward then grimaced, remembering his leg that he'd already pushed too far today, and stopped. 'I understand why you don't let people close, why you don't want to talk about your past. But you must know life goes on. And that doesn't mean you've forgotten Joe. No one would ever expect you to. It doesn't mean you can't be happy again. You can't deny the chemistry we have. You don't need to push me away but I need to know whether you want to take this attraction we have further or whether you want me to walk away now.'

'It's not about what I want. It's about you.'

'How?'

'Chemistry doesn't matter. Not when I'm everything you detest.'

'I don't get it.'

'You detest people valuing money over everything else.'

'You think that's what you did?'

'It's exactly what I did. We could've sold the house, I should've changed my work plans. I should've put Joe first.'

'Could've, should've. Two of the least useful words in the English language. Who do you know who would have done those things?'

She shrugged. 'It doesn't matter who would or would not have done those things. The only thing that matters is that I didn't. And because of that Joe died.'

She was right to doubt him. Because deep down, under his genuine reaction of wanting to comfort her, of knowing it hadn't been her fault, a voice of doubt was niggling and whispering in his head. As a doctor and a mother, if she'd been at home, she would have known. She could have diagnosed him correctly. And Joe might have lived. That was probably true, but that didn't make it her fault. It didn't mean she *should have* been at home.

She was watching him closely, almost with the studied concentration of someone making an objective assessment. 'You agree with me.' It wasn't a question and he was sure he could feel relief in her voice—relief at the thought he was agreeing it was her fault? Did she need to punish herself so much that she only felt comfortable hearing pronouncements of guilt?

It floored him. 'I agree that if you were home, you might have known sooner how sick Joe was, but—'

'And at some level, you know that if we hadn't been so focussed on the dream house, the all-consuming careers, it would've turned out very differently.'

'Phoebe, you're putting words into my mouth. And how do any of us ever know what would have happened? "If only" are two very complicating words. If you'd stayed at home, maybe something else would've happened that you'd have had no control over. You don't know.'

'But I know what did happen.'

'And because of that, you don't deserve a life?

Haven't you lost enough?' He counted them off on his fingers. 'Your baby, your marriage and, I gather, your home and your job. And goodness knows what else. When will you have done your penance?'

She'd stood now, and her face was pale as she faced him. 'I saw the look in your eyes when I told you. You're trying to tell yourself it's not true but, admit it, you're thinking it, too. If I'd been at home, if I hadn't put money first, it wouldn't have happened. It's my fault.'

'Phoebe—'

She held up one hand. 'No, Max, please, don't say anything. That's my story, my life and I have to live with it. I don't want to talk any more. If you'll excuse me, I think I'll get changed out of my bathers and go to bed.'

And she went. But Max was blowed if he was going to let that be the end of it. She'd opened up to him, told him her history and obviously expected that tale to spell the end to any relationship or friendship they might have. He wasn't going to prove her right.

Ten minutes later he followed her upstairs, stopping outside her closed door and knocking. 'Phoebe, I've brought you a coffee.'

She opened the door. She had changed out of her swimsuit but the singlet and short pyjama bottoms she now wore didn't cover much more of her. Max concentrated on keeping his gaze at her eye level.

'Can I come in? There's something I need to say.'

For a moment he thought she was going to take the mug and close the door but she stepped back, opening the door wider to let him in. She sat, curled up at the head of her bed, tucked among her pillows. Max put the coffee-cup on her bedside table and sat at the opposite end of the bed. He wanted so badly to take her in his arms, to offer comfort, but he knew she'd push him away. The protective shield she had around herself was so strong it was almost tangible. He tried to comfort her with words instead.

'I wasn't judging you. It was an awful thing that happened but, no matter what I think, it won't change anything. You were doing what you thought was the right thing for your family at the time. Fate intervened, everything went pear-shaped and now you carry those scars. And just because we can't see them, it doesn't make them any less painful but doesn't mean your life is over. Aren't you afraid of what you might miss out on if you refuse to let go of the past?'

'No.' Her answer was immediate. 'I'm afraid of what might go wrong.'

'And tomorrow? What does that hold for you?'

'I don't know.'

'What if we take a rain-check on dinner?' He stood. 'Then tomorrow we start again, no secrets, just a healthy curiosity about where this might lead us. Any chance we could do that?'

She looked at him long and hard. Then, to his surprise, she nodded. 'I'd like that.' And although there was still doubt in her voice, when she raised her face to his, he saw there was a glimmer of hope in her eyes.

'I'm out,' Max said as he threw his cards into the centre of the table where they landed beside a pile of betting chips.

'Do you want to borrow some cash?' Ned asked.

'No, I'm right. I've lost enough already. I reckon I'll head home.'

'I've never seen anyone look so happy about losing!' Ned said as he and Max left Tiny's place, leaving the others to their poker game.

'There's more to life than money, mate.'

Max caught Ned's sideways glance. 'I guess there is.'

'So you want to tell me why you can drop a couple of hundred bucks and still look like you won the lottery?'

'Life's good. Work's good and my leg's on the mend. I've got no complaints.'

'And Phoebe?'

'I don't think she's got any complaints either.'

'So it's happening between you?' Ned asked.

'Looks that way. Early days still, it's all pretty casual.'

'She's not the sort of who does "casual". Why do you think I've left her alone?'

'Don't stress. She told me herself she lives one day at a time. She's not asking for a commitment and I'm not offering one.'

'Don't mess her around, that's all I'm saying.'

'Don't worry about it, mate. We're both where we want to be. She told me what happened with her son—'

'She told you about Joe?' Ned didn't try to hide his surprise.

'Yeah. And I understand where she's at. She's cautious. I'm not going to pressure her.'

'Are you sure that's not what you find so attractive about her? She doesn't want a serious relationship so you're not in any danger of finding yourself in one?'

'Why would you ask me that?'

'Because the Max I know has never been close to getting into a serious relationship. Between your mum pressuring you about your career and your Canadian chick pulling a fast one on you, you've been every bit as much a bachelor as me. You've just taken it further and ignored any feminine attention, unlike me. Until Phoebe. Is it really that Phoebe's got something no one else has? Maybe she's not the only one running scared.'

'You think I'm only attracted to her because there's no chance she'd return the interest?'

'That's what I'm wondering.'

'I'm telling you, we're OK. We're in the same place, no secrets and just enjoying taking things slowly.'

'Don't believe it. Women are far more complicated than us males. Just be sure you know what you're doing. If she's told you about Joe, she's more serious about you than you think. I don't want her to get hurt, she's been through enough.'

'I have no intention of hurting her.' He held up three fingers, holding his little finger down with his thumb. 'Scout's honour.'

'Max, if there's one thing I know, neither of us are Scouts.' Ned punched him lightly on the arm, back to his good-natured best, yet Max knew him well enough to heed his warning. Hurt Phoebe and he'd be answering to Ned.

'It's mine as much as yours and there's no price you can put on it that would make me sell,' Phoebe hissed down the phone line as Max paused on the kitchen threshold, hesitating when he heard her on the phone.

She had her back to him but he didn't need to see her face to know she was far from happy. She was silent now, listening, but he knew she didn't like what she was hearing. He wasn't sure he liked what he was hearing either. It sounded like an argument over money or possessions. He'd rather listen to fingernails being scraped down a blackboard than be privy to such a discussion.

'You can rave on about property values as much as you want, I'm not selling.' She slammed down the receiver and turned, catching Max just as he was about to go.

'Hi.' She raised a smile, crossing the room to press a kiss on his cheek. Both gestures seemed forced.

'Everything OK? Someone hassling you?'

She shrugged, 'Fine, and not really.'

'You're edgy. Sure you're OK?' As she started to answer, he held up a hand. 'Let me guess, it's nothing a run won't fix.'

'Am I that predictable already?' Her laugh was more relaxed this time, but he still had a tight feeling in his gut. He really hadn't liked what he'd heard. 'I'm actually not thinking about running, I've already been today, but luckily that bread dough…' she waved a hand at the mound of dough on the kitchen table '…is crying out to be pounded. Want to help?'

She'd sidestepped the topic and it was clear she knew she'd done it. She hadn't quite met his eyes when she'd laughed. And now?

'That's a mighty beating you're administering,' he said, his voice mild as he watched her pummel her fist repeatedly into the pasty white mound on the table top.

She blew flour and a few wisps of her fringe off her nose and fixed him with a look. 'I might as well tell you since I can tell you're dying to know. That was Adam, my ex. He wants to buy my share of an investment property we have with two of our friends.'

'He's gone back on your property agreement?'

'Not exactly.' She shrugged. 'When we stitched up the property, we left that place aside. It was rented out and pretty much paid for itself so it wasn't a drain for any of us financially. Now he's doing well in his specialty, he wants a beach house and he can afford to buy me out. He knows I can't buy him out.'

'What do you want?'

She shrugged and gave the dough a final whack before she started kneading it, none too gently.

'Come on, other than leaving permanent indentations in the table, what do you want?'

'I don't want to sell.'

'He's not offering you enough?'

Again the shrug. 'It's a fair price.'

'You want more? Or you don't want to let go of the last connection with him?' It came out rougher than he'd meant, but every bit as blunt as he felt. Either scenario didn't augur well for *them*. Neither did the fact she'd 'forgotten' to mention she still owned a place with her ex when she'd said all their finances were sorted.

'You're angry with me. Why?' She didn't stop kneading, didn't make eye contact, and he'd bet she knew exactly what the issue was.

'I'm not angry,' he said, knowing the words were ridiculous even as he said them. Of course he was angry! 'But I'm wondering why you made it sound the other night like everything was resolved with Adam.' Which she had, in no uncertain terms—and now this! 'You said you'd sold your house, split it fifty-fifty, and you were OK about the divorce. Any reason why you didn't mention you still owned a place with him? You said you were amicable, friends even. You didn't mention anything about yelling down the phone at each other about a mystery property portfolio.'

'Actually, I was the only one yelling, and it's the first time it's happened. He just pushed my buttons, that's all.' She was pulling the dough into long stretches now, then folding it back on itself. The rapid changes in its shape echoed the rapid changes in Phoebe—just who was the real

Phoebe? 'And it's not a portfolio, it's one lousy beach house, and I didn't tell you about the beach house because it hasn't been an issue.'

'Until now.'

'Looks that way.' Grabbing a tin, she eased the dough into shape inside it, and left it by the switched-on oven to rise while she turned her back to him and washed her hands.

He waited for her to flick the tap and dry her hands before he spoke again.

'Can you tell me why it's an issue?'

'Can you tell me why you need to know?'

'I don't like secrets.'

'You think I'm keeping another secret from you? I don't want to sell to Adam because I'm rubbing my hands together, thinking of more money, is that it?'

'I don't know what to think.'

'I do. I think Ned's warning hints to me were right, not that I paid any attention at the time— you seemed too nice.' Ned had been warning them both independently? He opened his mouth to defend himself then closed it again. Had Ned been right about him? Or had he, Max, been right about Phoebe? 'I think you've leapt to a conclusion about me as an excuse to pull away. Now I'm not running scared of getting involved with you, you're the one who's scared. So you've latched on to the first excuse you can find to wedge some distance between us. Styling me a money-grabber is one way to do it. Somewhat hurtful, given what I confided in you about my past, about my guilt over putting work and so on before my baby. Or are you going with your theory that I can't let Adam go?'

'I haven't said—'

'You didn't need to. We've both said more than enough. But perhaps if you'd been less quick to offer me your explanations, I might have been inclined to share a few other possibilities with you.'

'And I take it you're not going to do that now.'

She sniffed and blinked a few times, making a show of wiping flour from her face. 'There's no point. You're so hung up on people taking you for a ride, keepings secrets from you. I could tell you every single thought in my head for the rest of eternity and you'd still convince yourself I'm keeping secrets.'

'The catch is, of course, that you were. You were keeping secrets, Phoebe. And you're right.

Now I'll never be sure when I ask you something if you are being truthful.'

'And you'll always be scared I'll jump out of my disguise and start chasing money, pulling you along with me. That's about it, isn't it, Max?'

'That's about it.'

'Then you can say I've got the issues if you want.' She was fumbling with the ties of her apron, looped around her waist, finally pulling it free and slipping it over her head. With a flourish she threw it down onto the table, which was still floury and covered with cooking utensils. She seemed not to notice. 'But the way I see it, one of us is ready to take a risk and love again.' She walked to the kitchen door and, with shoulders back and head high, met his eyes with a challenge in her own. 'And that person is not you.'

Running was all very well as a coping mechanism, but when your thoughts were going faster than your legs, it was impossible to outpace them. And it was escape she was looking for, thought Phoebe as she admitted defeat and headed for home. At least physical exhaustion would help her sleep tonight. Maybe. She'd seen almost every hour arrive on her digital clock last night.

Her parents' house lay between her and her own cottage. There was her dad tending his grape-vines, there was Ned working a little distance from him, lending a hand, as he so often did. She could hear her mum singing inside the house, which meant she was either cooking or stitching something. The local Rotary club had been pleased to welcome her mum into their fold. With her endless energy and creative talents, she could practically produce the goods for a fundraiser single-handed. She stopped where she was, on the crest of the last low hill, and eased into her stretches, watching the two men at their work, lis-tening to her mother's easy voice dip and turn its way through a medley, feeling the morning sunshine on her face and the soft breeze cooling her limbs, shiny with sweat.

She was lucky to have all this—her home, her family, her friends, her work. She knew that. But the time had come, finally, when she knew she wanted more. She'd been hiding here, hiding among people who loved her and so wouldn't push her to face the world until she was ready.

She could let Max's attitude to her stand as a warning not to venture into the world again, but he'd woken something in her, stirred her desire to live again, not just exist. And so now she knew she wanted more.

And not only that.

Now she knew she deserved it.

Which in itself was nothing short of a miracle.

That was the only miracle coming her way that morning, though, Phoebe realised as she entered the house ten minutes later. She heard the music before she'd entered the house, of course, and the beauty of the song made her hope for one, mad moment that this was Max's way of building bridges, through his music, telling her it was not over. It *was* a beautiful song, a lament really, and although she knew it had been written before they'd met, the words could have been speaking to her alone. Bitter-sweet, that was how it made her feel, and as she listened to the chorus, she chanced a guess that it was called that, too. She hadn't heard this song before, but it was Max's voice, so this must be the set of tracks he'd been waiting for, the latest mix for him to approve.

She had hardly seen him, not to have a proper conversation with at any rate, since their disastrous meeting over the dough. So disastrous, in fact, she'd simply not been able to touch the finished loaf. The gorgeous rich smell of freshly baked bread had made her feel nauseous. Ned had scored the entire loaf. Now, standing at the threshold of the lounge, the door partly ajar, she couldn't see Max but she could see his reflection in the big round mirror on the wall. He was sitting on a chair in front of the CD player, scribbling notes. It wasn't the image of a man preparing himself to win back his would-be lover. It was the image of a man totally focussed on his music.

The track ended and she turned to leave, embarrassed to be watching him at work, observing unannounced a private moment. The floorboards creaked and without the cover of the music he heard her. 'Phoebe?'

Shaking her head, she gave up hope of a subtle retreat and stepped into the room. It was her room after all, she needn't be embarrassed about being there. Something more was required than a simple 'hello'.

'That was lovely. Really, a beautiful song. Did

you write it?' If she had been interviewing for a job, she'd sound perfect, but the formal tone of her voice highlighted how strained things were now between them.

He stood, stretching his limbs with the languor of a sleek cat. He looked not sad but serious—thinking about his music? His mind was somewhere other than there with her, so the song hadn't made him think with regret about their lost chance.

That thought made her feel unbearably sad and she looked away, out the window, to find solace in the gardens and hills beyond the house.

'Thanks,' he said, answering her in a manner as formal as hers had been. They were now looking in each other's general direction but both taking care not to meet the other's gaze. 'I did write it. A few licks are still out, but overall I'm happy with it.'

'I wanted to say—'

He spoke at the same time. 'I wanted to—' Then when they both stopped, embarrassed, he added, 'You go first.'

'I wanted to clear the air. If we're both living here, working in the same station, I need to do that.'

He nodded but gave her no other encouragement that he at least wanted this, too.

'And to do that, I need to tell you there was another reason I didn't mention the beach house. I didn't think it was an issue, so it didn't cross my mind for more than a moment anyway.' She swallowed, nervous. She was about to lay her soul bare when she knew there was less than a drop of hope it would change anything. 'I also didn't want to think about it, not that night we had dinner. It was such a lovely evening. I just wanted that one night imagining what it would have been like to meet you if all the things that have happened hadn't. Do you understand?'

'I think so.'

'I wanted to pretend that we were just two people who'd met, and something had started, and I wasn't carrying the hurt and the loss I am. I wanted to feel for one night who I might have been without that. I know it's not possible. But I wanted it.'

'I can understand that.'

'But it makes no difference to how you feel.' Why she said the words for him, she didn't know. Maybe she didn't want to see his face, his words as he told her again it was over.

He shook his head slowly, and finally they

made eye contact. Now he looked sad, which tugged at her heart. 'Thank you for telling me but, no, we've gone too far now to go back. I have something for you, though.' He turned and picked up a CD cover from the coffee-table. 'Like I said, it's not finished, but it's almost there. I did promise you a copy of the next mix.'

So he was offering it not to share his music but to underline the point that he, at least, kept his word. He could be trusted. Maybe he didn't mean the message to be as direct as that, but she got it all the same.

She stepped forward and took it, glancing at the simple clear cover and the CD inside, on which a number of song titles, including 'Bitter-sweet', the track she'd just heard, were scrawled in his handwriting.

'Thank you.' A nervous swallow, wanting to prolong this conversation and knowing there was no comfortable way to do it. 'I think I heard "Bitter-sweet" playing when I came in.'

He nodded, and didn't add any more. If that song made him think of her, he wasn't letting her know it. She fished again. 'It was lovely. Is it the one you're happiest with?'

A short shake of his head and then as an after-thought, he said, '"Coming Home". You haven't heard it before.' And he didn't offer to play it for her now. He didn't elaborate further, and she took the offered CD. Their fingers brushed for no more than a moment, but it was in that one moment she realised what she hadn't quite accepted before.

She was in love with Max.

Her heart could be whole again with him. Not the same as it had been before, Joe was always part of her heart now, but it could be a loving heart, alive with hopes and dreams.

It was, in fact, a loving heart even now. Love had seeped into its fibres, but it was not a heart she could share with the man who had allowed her to love again. He wouldn't be singing his gorgeous songs to her, he wouldn't be writing them with caressing thoughts of her in mind. The brief chapter in which they'd shared one another's lives had ended.

They looked into each other's eyes once more, sadness reflected in both, and she knew it wasn't sadness only because she'd failed to be totally honest with him. He wasn't ready to risk his own heart again, as she'd suggested to him before.

She nodded, she couldn't quite manage a smile, and left the room. To be alone was what she needed now. She had to go somewhere by herself and digest the revelation.

The revelation she was in love with Max.

Her heart had only just come alive again, or so it felt. She wasn't going to bury it, try and stop the pain she was feeling. Rather, she'd celebrate it, because it was proof at least that she had started on life again. There was hope. Not for her and Max, and she wouldn't let him see how terribly much that hurt, but for her there was hope. And she'd cling to that, shore up her courage with the belief there was something for her in this life after all.

It just wasn't going to be what she wanted most.

CHAPTER NINE

BETWEEN an angry crack at him from Ned over Phoebe and Phoebe's stubborn refusal to let Max see his rebuff had had any affect on her at all, Max was convinced he was less than welcome at the cottage. Other than seeing her briefly to give her the CD, they hadn't spoken. She'd explained about the beach house, about why she hadn't told him before, but it didn't make any difference. He guessed she was angry with him—maybe with good reason, maybe not. Either way, making himself scarce around the cottage seemed best for everyone concerned.

Max was no different to any other self-respecting firefighters. He knew when to make use of the bunks at the station.

And so he'd stayed on shift longer than he needed to a few times this week, covered for a bloke whose wife and son had gastro, caught up on his admin work, brought forward four meetings to fill in another few hours here and there and relieved others from their shifts hours before he had been due at work. All in all, it had made him a very popular acting station officer.

What he hadn't done had been to leave any time to process what had happened with Phoebe. And why.

His brief moments of reflection had suggested he'd been out of line. But he also knew Phoebe had been right when she'd said he was looking for a reason not to get involved. And the way he'd handled things between them, he had not getting involved in the bag. Why go undoing it all?

Common sense told him to leave things well enough alone.

Emotion was insisting he'd be an idiot to do that.

Emotion had him straining to hear who it was each time he heard a voice in the station. Emotion left him dull with disappointment each time it wasn't Phoebe.

So after three days of playing hide-and-seek with both his feelings and the object of his affections he decided to make a phone call to the woman who had messed with his head so brilliantly four years ago.

If he had to suffer for her sins, if he had to now suck at relationships because she'd been born without morals, he could at least remind her that she was as ethically bankrupt as she'd left him emotionally impoverished.

After all, he thought as he sat, hiding away in the station officer's office, misery loved company. And right now he was acing misery.

Max was halfway through dialling Lisbette's number in Canada before he realised what he was doing. He knew Lisbette's number by heart, as well he should. It had been his number as well for two years and he'd paid every single bill for it. And every other bill. But halfway through dialling, the number had morphed into another string of digits. Another number he knew by heart, a number that was also now his. But the woman who answered calls to that number would not be speaking in French. Not beyond a few badly attempted sentences, at any rate. She wouldn't be batting her eyelids to squeeze yet more money out of him for more frivolous expenses. And she wouldn't be pretending to love him so he'd cough up his hard-earned dollars and provide free babysitting for her son.

And suddenly he saw what he'd done.

And what he needed to do.

It wasn't Lisbette he needed to talk to. What would he say? Nothing. There was nothing he needed to say to her he hadn't already said many, many times to his empty room in the middle of the night. She had no power over him, not any more, and he wouldn't go on conducting himself as if she did.

He'd been a different person then. Naïve, trusting, willing to love and be loved. And there was nothing intrinsically wrong with that, with any of it. There was also no reason to be afraid he'd make those same mistakes again. They were the allowable mistakes of youth. If he refused to trust his older—hopefully wiser, but he couldn't vouch for that—instincts now, he would be laying far too much blame on the shoulders of his younger self.

At the very least he owed Phoebe an apology. At the very best she'd accept it and agree they could start over, see if their pasts couldn't be meshed together so they could look towards a shared future.

He was determined to speak to Phoebe that night. He replaced the receiver but the phone rang immediately. He snatched it up, knowing it wouldn't be Phoebe but wishing otherwise.

It was a call from head office in Adelaide. Max swallowed his disappointment as he took the call, jotting down notes and trying to make room in his head for the information he was getting. Fires that had started yesterday in the bush north of Sydney, New South Wales, were now raging out of control and threatening hundreds of homes on the outskirts of the city. They were desperately short of manpower and interstate firefighters were being asked to volunteer. Would he ask for volunteers among the crew?

He would.

He'd even offer his own services. His leg was not yet healed but he wouldn't be in the line of fire, so to speak, he'd be co-ordinating a crew so his injury wouldn't be an impediment.

He had four hours before the plane left to organise covering officers, rearrange the station rosters, liaise with the city station and get to the airport.

Four hours to do all that and one other important task that couldn't be left any longer.

With the determination of a man with a newly bequeathed mission, he churned his way through this list with exactly forty minutes to spare, although that calculation erred on the side of generosity, assuming he caught every light between here and the airport. So, at a stretch, forty minutes to head for home in the hope of catching Phoebe and putting things straight. Or at least let her know he wanted to.

A long shot, he knew, but it was better than nothing.

'Adam!'

Her ex-husband—soon to be ex, she reminded herself—was standing on the threshold of the cottage, overnight bag and briefcase in hand, looking unsure of his welcome. She'd hoped it was Max. Not that he'd be knocking, he had a key, but as far as she knew, he hadn't been home for at least two nights. So she'd hoped. 'Hi, Phoebe, it's been a long time. If you don't count our fun chat a few days back.'

Adam saw her glance at his bag and must have interpreted her suspicions accurately, adding with a cautious smile, 'I'm not here to stay. I've stopped off on my way through to Perth for a conference.' He glanced beyond her, inside. 'Can I come in? I haven't come to browbeat you, just to talk.'

Phoebe stepped back and motioned him inside. She waited until they were seated in the living room. Adam had declined any offer of a drink before she'd even made one. 'I've been debating ringing you to apologise. I didn't mean to yell. I don't know what came over me.'

'It's OK. Believe me, I know how tough this has all been, and I imagine the news about Karen and I getting engaged was hard to hear. I'm sorry if that's the case, but we've always been truthful with each other, and you were going to find out. I thought it'd be better coming from me.'

'That's not why I was upset!'

'Really?'

She made a cross with her forefinger on her chest. 'Truly.' Then she smiled, maybe her first real smile all week. 'It was much pettier than that, which is why I haven't rung you yet. I was embarrassed.' There was no reason not to tell Adam what had been behind her reaction. She had more than enough tension with Max to want any more. 'I realised afterwards I was scared that if you bought me out, then you'd own the place with Margot and Glen and I'd be excluded, that they wouldn't be my friends any more.'

'I could've saved you the trauma if you'd stopped yelling and not hung up on me so fast. Or if you'd at least given Margot a call.'

'Because?'

'Because I've offered to buy them out, too. Or rather this idea to buy you all out came from a comment they made a few weeks ago. They want to open a picture-framing business and they need the start-up capital. They mentioned the beach house but were obviously uncomfortable about pushing for a sale. I imagine they were concerned about how you and I would feel.' Adam was smiling, a teasing light in his eyes. 'With good reason, I might add, given your reaction.'

Phoebe squirmed. 'Not about selling the house per se.'

'I'm teasing, I know it's been hard for you.'

She reached over to touch him lightly on the arm. 'On us both. But we're looking to the future now. Right?'

He chucked her under the chin. 'Not the one we

planned on, but maybe we can both make it count for something, anyway.'

'Does it ever get any easier for you?'

'Do I ever forget?'

She nodded.

'No. I don't imagine that ache will ever go away. And would we want it to? That's what tells me every day how much I loved our little guy. That's the hole that nothing else will ever fill, but that makes me more terrified of never feeling that type of love again than of losing it again.'

She was quiet for a moment. They'd never spoken about this, not fully. Their grief hadn't turned them against each other. They hadn't blamed and hurled their anger at each other, only at themselves. So they'd simply stood by while their marriage had dissolved, quietly, without words. How strange that now she'd finally let her heart feel again, now the words would come. And now, she sensed, Adam needed this conversation, this clearing of the unspoken, as much as she did. Blinking, steeling herself to ask the question that would show the burden she herself had carried all these years, she said, 'Do you still feel guilty?'

He looked at her, took her hand, and his eyes

were damp. 'If there was anything I could do to bring him back, I would.' He sat quietly for a moment then went on, 'I've forgiven myself, though, which is what you're asking, I think.' She nodded. 'How did we know what was going to happen? Would we make the same choices now? Probably not, but no one gets the benefit of another go so no one should judge themselves by the yardstick of hindsight. I did that for a long time and then at some point I stopped. I'm not sure how or when or why. Maybe when I met Karen,' he said, a note of pride in his voice making Phoebe envious. How lucky Adam was to have found love again, to have it returned! 'And you? Have you forgiven yourself?'

'I think I have,' said Phoebe, realising as she said the words that it was true. 'But only now, only in the immediate aftermath of our entirely unsatisfactory phone call.' She shuddered at the memory. Max had been noticeable only by his absolute absence since then. 'I've been seeing someone, and when he heard us on the phone, or rather heard me, he pretty much decided I was a shrew screaming about money.' She shrugged. 'It was what it sounded like.'

'You're involved with someone? Margot mentioned she had her suspicions but didn't want to pry. What happened?'

'I *was* involved. That phone call, combined with what I'd told him about going back to work to pay our mortgage, convinced him I'm the money-hungry type of woman he abhors.'

'Harsh.'

'Maybe. It's what it sounded like and I didn't put him straight. He's got some things to sort out and right now I'm just peeping over the edge at a new life. I don't have the energy to deal with that. I think,' she said slowly, 'I simply couldn't. But it was when I felt he was judging me that suddenly things clicked into place and I realised I didn't need to punish myself any more. Somehow my world has shifted and I know I don't have to bear the blame any more. It's crippled me for the past three years. That's enough.'

'Do you mind if I ask you something?'

She nodded.

'Are you sure it's over, that he has judged you? Are you sure you're not pushing him away because you're scared of getting involved?' She started to speak but he placed a hand on her arm, silently asking her to wait a moment. 'You shut us all out after we lost Joe. Not just me, all our friends. Margot is only part of your life still because she knew you better than most and she knew not to take all your rebuffs, the unreturned phone calls, the excuses not to accept invitations, as anything other than grief talking. And as for me, you had to keep a dialogue with me to some extent, due to the house and so on. But you carved everyone else off from your life so absolutely it was scary. Are you sure you're not doing the same thing now?'

'I've been a lousy friend. Lousy at life, really. I know.'

'That's not what I'm saying. I'm not judging you, I'm not saying anything remotely like that.' He'd pulled her into his arms, and she let him hold her, as she hadn't been able to when they'd lost Joe. Until Max, no one had been allowed to hold her since then. Now she found she could let Adam, and that there was comfort in it, the comfort of someone who wasn't asking for anything, just offering a moment of solace to a sore heart.

* * *

Max wasn't sure what he was going to say. 'Sorry' would feature prominently, but other than that the words would come, he knew. So on the drive, and as he walked into the house, he concentrated only on the image of Phoebe's face, not willing to consider she might not be at the house when he arrived or, if she was, she might not be willing to listen to anything he had to say.

It didn't occur to him that he would be the one who would be listening.

But, having entered the house silently, focussed only on staying calm, he heard Phoebe's voice—satisfaction welling in him that she was there—and then another voice. It was one he didn't know, a man's voice, which gave him no cause for panic, only frustration that now he'd have to find a way to convince Phoebe to excuse herself so he could say what he needed to say.

As he approached the living room, their words became discernible, and as he listened, if it wasn't panic bubbling up inside him, it wasn't mere frustration either.

It was something more akin to shock.

The shock intensified as he reached the door

way and found he couldn't see Phoebe, but he could see her back in the mirror on the wall. She was in someone's arms, held against a man's chest, his arm tight around her shoulders, her head nestled on his chest, and the man was stroking her hair in a gesture of such intimacy and caring Max froze, unable to leave, as he knew he should.

'Your heart broke,' said the male voice. Adam? 'Mine did, too. What I'm asking you is if there's not a chance now of a new beginning? We lost Joe, we'll never forget him.' Yes, definitely Adam. Max stopped where he was, close to the door leading into the living room. Adam went on, 'But you and I, Phoebe, we didn't die. And if you're starting to think that maybe you do have a right not to just keep living but to actually have a life, then are you sure it's over?'

The voice was soft, a caress, full of tenderness and caring and love. So he'd been right to fear after all. Phoebe hadn't wanted to sell the beach house because that would cut the last tie with Adam. She still cared for him. Why else would Adam be here, holding Phoebe? Why else would he sound as if he loved her and be asking for another chance? He, Max, shouldn't be here. He'd been right. But he *was* here, and he found he couldn't move, just couldn't. Like watching a car crash, he had to hear her answer, see it through so he'd know how it ended, even though there wasn't a thing he could do to change the outcome.

So he stood frozen, for all intents, on the spot. He'd come here wanting her answer to his question—could they start again, in some way?—and he was waiting for her answer now, but it wasn't to a question of his asking. It was to her ex-husband's question.

Just like Lisbette.

No, not just like Lisbette. Lisbette had deliberately pretended she'd had feelings she hadn't, for her own ends. One thing he knew, and that was that Phoebe hadn't orchestrated any of this. She'd been confused, frightened and as brave as anyone could be in the face of the devastation of the death of a child. But blameless as he suddenly knew her to be, that didn't equate necessarily to the outcome he wanted.

So the words that had been a shifting cloud in his mind as he'd driven here, assuming they'd take form when the moment arose, he now heard being uttered by another, a man who, no doubt, knew Phoebe much better than he did.

And now there were two of them, two men, and he was feeling more ill with dread than he ever had, waiting for Phoebe's reply to the question— 'Are you sure it's over?'

'You're obviously unsure,' Adam said now. 'It's taking you ages to answer so I'll ask you in another way. Are you in love with Max?'

In shock, Max shifted his weight before he thought about it and the floorboards gave the tiniest creak, too small for Phoebe and Adam to hear hopefully, but it reminded him he was effectively eavesdropping. Not attractive. Not something he had ever done before. And yet, as much as he knew he should, he couldn't leave without hearing her answer. In the last few minutes he'd gone from being full of hope to despair at finding her in Adam's arms and thinking Adam and Phoebe still loved one another. Now hope had been resurrected, and Phoebe was holding it in her hands. Would she dash it at her feet or hand him the gift he hadn't known until so very recently he'd wanted?

'No,' she said. 'I thought I could be, at one

stage, but I'm not. I couldn't love someone who didn't trust me and was always on the lookout for me to mess up. You and I didn't make it, but trust was never an issue. And you can't love someone who doesn't trust you. So I don't. I don't love Max.'

Her answer sliced through him and he turned on his heel towards his room, not caring if the old floorboards gave him away by creaking. But the unpredictable old house was in favour of his clandestine departure and there was no sound, nothing so much as hinted he was present as he grabbed the few items he'd need for the interstate trip.

The shock was immediate. And when the shock wore off, he knew it was going to hurt. A lot.

Max left as quietly as he'd come, pausing for a moment to look back at the cottage that had come to seem like home in such a short time. Strange how things turn out, he thought, half-numb, as he took in the scene. He'd come home today with a new understanding of what Phoebe could mean to him; he was leaving with the knowledge that although there had been a chance for them, he'd missed it.

He knew this was the last time he'd come here thinking he was coming home. Next time he'd be coming to pack his gear to move. He couldn't stay here any more—neither of them would be comfortable.

For all our planning, he thought, for all our hopes, life can rearrange itself in the space of a moment. That's all it took. When he'd come home today, he'd been imagining living here with Phoebe, not as housemates but together, as a couple. It had been a vague plan, not yet tangible, but it had involved him applying for a permanent transfer to Hahndorf Station.

And because he was numb, all he could think was how strange it was, how things turned out sometimes. And how cruel that life should whisk Phoebe beyond his reach just when he'd realised how much he wanted her in his life.

He'd been disappointed that volunteering to go to Sydney had meant he'd be spending the next few days away from Phoebe, and his absence would delay their fresh start. But he could see now he'd made some rather big assumptions. He'd just assumed they'd have a chance. But it looked as though he'd been wrong.

At least the round-the-clock work, fighting the NSW fires, wouldn't allow him time to think.

They were trained to not allow emotions or personal affairs to distract them from work.

But when the fires were over? Then he'd just have to use that same training to forget how, for one mad moment, he'd seen a different future for himself.

'People deal with things differently. Who can say there's a right way? Your heart broke. Mine did, too. What I'm asking you is if there's not a chance now of a new beginning?'

The irony wasn't lost on Phoebe. Her soon-to-be ex-husband was reassuring her—yet neither of them had been able to play that role when they'd needed it most. The fault didn't lie with Adam alone, she knew that. Their marriage had been strained before she'd fallen pregnant. Exhausted from long hours at work and differing schedules, they'd neglected to cherish the time they had had together. Joe had bound them together again but the irony was they'd had even less time for their relationship.

And when Joe died, and they'd been left seeing each other—really seeing each other, for the first time in a long time—through the screen of their grief, it had become clear: they no longer had a future together. Whatever ties had bound them together in the past hadn't been strong enough to clear a path through the cloud of their loss and let them lean on each other. The consolation Adam was offering now they hadn't been able to offer each other at the time of their greatest need. Somehow they'd both seen it. It hadn't needed long conversations or nights of recriminations or regrets. They'd both simply known they hadn't been meant to walk through life by each other's sides.

They'd quietly drifted away from one another, made new lives.

Half-lives. For her, anyway, until the clouds had cleared temporarily with the arrival of Max.

Yet now Adam was here, reassuring her, and there was no confusion about his role: a friend, for old times' sake, offering support. And something in her had shifted significantly, because she could accept him in that role. It felt safe to let him in.

So maybe that brief escape from her half-life of sequestering her emotions, of hiding from the world, had done some good after all?

'We lost Joe and we'll never forget him. But you and I, Phoebe, we didn't die. And if you're starting to think that maybe you do have a right to not just keep living but to actually have a life, then are you sure it's over?'

Was she sure? She stood still for a while, thinking. If she could change the way things had turned out, would she? If she could seize the fading rays of that brief explosion of sunshine into her life, would she?

This was a meaningless exercise, this game of 'what if'. Life didn't work that way. You didn't get to go back, change the way things happened, but if she indulged in a flight of fancy…

Raising her head a little to look Adam in the eye and answer his question, she thought she saw a flash of movement in the mirror. Ned? Max? She'd heard nothing, no door opening, no car pulling up. She waited a moment more, straining to hear, but the old house, which tended to creak and groan, was quiet.

'You're obviously unsure, it's taking you ages to answer so I'll ask you in another way. Are you in love with Max?'

Phoebe knew the answer to that but that didn't mean she had to embrace public humiliation. Risk the truth or stay safe with a lie? The tiniest of creaks from the hallway decided her.

'No,' she said, daring fate to show her for a liar. 'I thought I could be, at one stage, but I'm not.'

After she had finished speaking, Phoebe still wasn't sure whether anyone had been there. But she had to know so she stood and strode to the door, opening it into the empty hallway.

Foolish was the word for how she felt when she returned to the couch where Adam was watching her, amused.

'I know you like the back of my hand, Phoebe. You always were the worst liar and I can see some things never change. I'll let you off the hook if you promise me you'll come to Sydney for Margot's birthday.'

'But that's only a few days away and I haven't booked a flight.'

Adam gave her a stern look, the sort that always got her back up, but before she could rebuke him he smiled and said, 'Margot's birthday has been on the same day for the last thirty years. It's hardly a surprise. She wants you there, Phoebe. Enough with the excuses. Please, come, for her sake.'

'If you think I'm hiding something then you're letting me go far too easily. What's the catch?'

'The catch is, Margot has much more skilled

ways of making you talk. She can take over where I've failed.'

She swatted him on the arm. 'I think it's fair enough that when I've just dipped my toe in the water of life, I'm not willing to be towed under. There's only so much a self-respecting woman can risk at any one time. And I include pride in that equation.'

'But how do you know who'll be there to catch you unless you throw yourself in and test the currents? And, to continue your analogy a step further, maybe if you did throw yourself in, you'd find the currents aren't so scary after all.'

'Did you get a philosophy degree since I last saw you?'

'Don't avoid the challenge: won't you take a chance?'

'To use your analogy,' she said dryly, 'I've only just stepped out on the jetty and I'm finding the thought of all that water under my feet terrifying enough, without entertaining thoughts of hurling myself over the edge.'

Adam laughed. 'Medicine's gain was philosophy's loss. I've just got time for a coffee if your hospitality extends that far.'

'Besides,' she muttered to herself as she led the way into the kitchen, looking for but seeing no signs that Max had been home, 'one of us would be bound to drown. Max because he wouldn't trust me not to drag him under, and me because I'd be too scared to reach out for help. Actually...' and she surprised herself by finding the irony amusing '...I'd be the one to drown in both those scenarios.'

'Chin up, Phoebes, you'll be OK. You're tougher than you look.' Adam put his arm around her shoulders, drawing her to his side before pulling her in against him in a proper hug. The sensation was comfortable and familiar but Phoebe's first thought was of the difference she felt within herself. Adam's hug brought with it no spark of attraction, unlike her reaction when Max had wrapped her in his arms. Adam was a friend, not a lover.

That place belonged to Max.

At least in her mind, if not in her reality.

'He's out there somewhere, that's what you're thinking, right?' Margot swished the curtains across the window, blocking the view, which wasn't a great loss as the skies across Sydney were, two days after Phoebe's arrival, still dark with smoke.

'Pardon?' Phoebe looked up from her magazine, pretending she hadn't just been looking out the window, thinking about Max.

'Ever since you arrived, you've been looking out there at least sixteen times an hour,' Margot said, hands on hips. 'Why don't you just ring him?'

'He's fighting fires.'

'And they don't have mobiles?'

Two-year-old Henry careered through the doorway, chubby arms held out, waiting to be picked up. Phoebe scooped him onto her lap before answering. 'Probably not.' She nuzzled her cheek against Henry's and wondered again how she was not only coping with spending time with Margot and Glen's children, she was even enjoying it. The pain about Joe was there, but she was nonetheless finding joy in the love of her friends' children.

Margot was watching her, waiting for more excuses. She gave her one. 'There's not a lot of time for personal calls in the middle of a major disaster zone,' she added, tickling Henry's tummy, stretched round like a drum after his impressive consumption at dinner.

'That's a defeatist attitude.'

'Maybe, but it's the one that'll keep me from doing something silly, like ringing a man who doesn't want to hear from me. And why would I do that,' she added, addressing Henry and shifting into baby talk that had Margot rolling her eyes, 'when I have this little guy lapping up my company?'

'Max doesn't want to hear from you based on what?'

'Based on the small fact he left the state to fight *your* bushfires and didn't leave me so much as a note—just passed on a message through Ned.'

'He would have been in a hurry. You should understand that, you're an ambulance chick.'

'Intensive care paramedic to you.'

'And another thing—are you going to let me listen to your CD?'

'I'm regretting ever telling you Max was in a band.' Phoebe sighed and aimed for a stern look but Henry, blowing a raspberry at that moment, brought her smile out. 'To quote my favourite movie, were you this much trouble at the Abbey?'

'Oh much, much more, Captain.'

'*Sir.*'

'There's only one thing for it,' Margot retorted, 'as soon as I get Yasmine and Henry to bed, we're watching it and you'll see I'm right. Glen's got work to do in his study so he won't interrupt. Are we on?'

'A night of love overcoming all obstacles is exactly what I need.'

Which wasn't exactly true.

What she really needed was Max.

The last thing Max wanted after four days of non-stop work in the midst of the bushfires was a bunch of TV cameras in his face. If vanity was an issue for him, he'd be hiding right now instead of standing here, unshaven, filthy and exhausted, with the stench of smoke ingrained into his skin.

'And live to air in five.' The sound technician mouthed the remaining numbers, counting down on his fingers.

The reporter beamed at the camera and introduced her segment. 'We're coming to you live from the Terrey Hills Civic Centre on the edge of Ku-ring-gai National Park where our emergency services men and women are battling nature in an effort to extinguish the mammoth bushfires raging out of control just over the hills you see behind me. A mobile command centre has been set up in the civic centre car park and it was here, before the break, that I chatted with some of our local heroes to find out what lies beneath the uniform, so to speak. We found a karate black belt, an artist and a mountain climber, and now we're getting up close and personal with Max Williams.'

She tittered at her introduction and Max disguised his disdain. Just. Turning disaster into fodder for prime-time viewing was not his idea of must-see TV.

She went on. 'Max is one of the many interstate firefighters who came to our aid.'

Was she batting her eyelashes at him? The power of a uniform, he thought savagely. Then she launched into her interview and the questions were almost word for word the same as those Max had just heard being asked of the previous interviewee. He'd bet his answers were similarly unimaginative.

She rushed on to the business end of the interview—her initial questions about the fire itself wasn't the angle she was after. 'But what we really want to know is, who is Max when he steps out of his uniform at the end of a long shift? What makes him tick? How does he relax? And…' she winked at the camera '…is there a special someone in his life?'

'Quick!' screeched Margot.

'What?' Phoebe came back into the living room, a block of chocolate tucked under one arm and a cup of tea in each hand, ready to watch their favourite movie. She deposited the stash on the coffee-table before looking at the TV. A blonde reporter was batting her eyelashes at the camera and fire trucks were coming and going in the background of what looked like a car park.

'It's Max, your Max, the twitty reporter just said so. They're at the mobile command centre.'

Phoebe plopped onto the couch, mouth agape as Max's image filled the screen. Broad shoul-dered and in uniform, the sight of him demanded attention despite the fact he was grimy, with dark rings under his eyes and at least a three-day growth darkening his jaw. His dishevelled ap-pearance added to the emergency services image of a hero, although, to Phoebe, he looked like he'd rather be anywhere other than in front of the camera.

'But what we really want to know is,' trilled the reporter as the camera cut back to her, 'who is Max when he steps out of his uniform at the end of a long shift? What makes him tick? How does he relax? And…' she winked at the camera '…is there a special someone in his life?'

The look on Max's face as the camera cut back to him had Margot hooting with laughter. 'He can't believe what he's hearing! And he's hot.' She kicked out a foot and got Phoebe in the side. 'Seriously, super-hot. You lucky, lucky girl.' And she sighed for good measure.

'Shh.'

'So, Max, put all the women out there out of their misery and tell us all—are you single?'

'Yes.' His answer was curt. It didn't deter the reporter but his sharpness sliced through Phoebe. There'd been not the slightest hesitation. Not even a tiny bit.

'And since I know you're too modest—'

'Because she's known him at least two minutes and she's talked almost non-stop through that time,' cut in Margot.

'Shh!' It was Phoebe's turn to shove Margot with a foot.

'We have a little treat for you.' Facing camera, she announced, 'We have an exclusive for those of you wondering what this particular firefighter gets up to when he's not saving lives.'

The look on Max's face as the music started said he'd had no idea this had been about to happen. And, Phoebe thought, he was not sure whether he should be running for cover as fast as he could or enjoying his band's moment of national TV coverage.

'This is the new track, "Coming Home", from Max's band, The Dirty Strangers,' she announced smugly, so smug anyone would think she'd written the song herself. The track played for ten seconds or so before she cut in again to announce the band's website details, leaving Phoebe reeling from the power of the song. She knew from the title it was the track he'd given her on the CD before he'd left Adelaide, but this was the first time she'd listened to it as she hadn't been able to bring herself to play it. Now she'd heard it, she was stunned. It was incredibly moving, and the song suited his voice perfectly. It was one he'd written, she knew, and she knew, too, how excited he'd been about it.

Having heard it, she knew she'd be playing it time after time in the following days, even if it did break her heart all over again. The track had now resumed, and a clip, presumably from the band's website, was being screened.

'Great,' she muttered to herself. Now she had to watch him perform, too, on top of being seduced by the music. The clip moved around the band in a live performance focussing on each band member in turn, a tight ensemble even to her un-schooled ears. But she wasn't watching the other band members, she was glued to the screen only for Max. He owned the stage, singing with con-viction, playing his guitar. He cut an impressive figure, even in his old jeans, T-shirt and bare feet.

It seemed a lifetime ago when they'd sung karaoke together, and when he'd serenaded her during his encore performance.

She'd fallen for him that night, she knew now. Fallen fast and hard and against all her intentions to stay safe, one step away from life and love.

Fallen in love, as it had turned out. Adam had seen right through her protestation that she didn't love Max. Someone with no emotional intelligence at all could have seen through it, she reflected ruefully.

The track came to a close. 'So he's gorgeous, talented and, when he's not saving lives, he writes amazing songs and sings like an angel,' added the reporter, now gazing with adoration up at Max, who towered over her.

'Damn him,' said Phoebe to Margot. 'He'll be dating someone else by next week and I'll be—' She didn't finish her sentence, breaking off to listen to Max.

'Uh—thanks,' Max said to the reporter, but his attention had been caught by something behind the camera. He was looking off into the distance and then suddenly alarm crossed his face and he grabbed the reporter and yelled, 'Get down.'

And then nothing.

The screen went blank for a few seconds and when the picture resumed the broadcast had cut to the studio where a surprised pair of presenters reassured the audience everything was fine before going to an ad break.

Phoebe was on her feet and heading for the door before her mind had processed what she'd just seen. Or not seen, depending on how she looked at it.

'What just happened and where are you going?' Margot asked.

'To find Max.'

'I'm coming, too.' She bolted off the couch, grabbed Phoebe by the arm, yelled to her husband where they were going and less than a minute later was reversing at some speed down the driveway.

'Margot?' said Phoebe as her friend swung the car a little too fast around the corner at the end of their street. 'Could you slow down? I'm just holding it together, telling myself Max will be all right, and you're not helping my nerves, driving like a maniac.'

The car slowed down noticeably, Margot giving an apologetic grimace. 'Sorry, it's been a while since I was in the midst of an unfolding love story.'

'He's going to be all right.' Phoebe looked out the window and fell silent. Houses flashed by and the streets turned into main roads as they left the outer suburbs and joined the evening traffic on the outbound freeway. Trying in vain to unclench her fists and the knot in her stomach, she could think only one thought.

If Adam were here now and asking if she loved Max, how very different her answer would be.

Pressing her forehead against the glass of the window, she repeated, 'He's going to be all right.'

And tried against all reason not to think about the last time she'd had this personal dialogue with a god who wasn't listening.

CHAPTER TEN

IT WAS twilight as they neared Terrey Hills but they knew they were almost there as the glow of lights in the sky became brighter and the screech of sirens grew louder. Following signs for the civic centre, they turned into the street and they could see the area was awash with emergency services personnel and lit up by myriad portable lighting sources.

The street was cordoned off and Margot pulled the car into a parking bay as close as she could get. 'Go, be brave.' She pulled Phoebe close for a hug. 'Don't back out now because you're afraid of getting hurt.'

She released her and when Phoebe spoke she was already half out of the car, on her way. 'I can honestly say my ego is not part of the equation. I just need to know Max is OK.'

And then she was gone, sprinting down the street,

disappearing in a glow of flashing lights, dodging through the crowd of firefighters, ambulance officers, police and a bustle of reporters being contained—just—behind a line of orange flags.

Somewhere, thought Margot, in that mayhem was the man who had brought Phoebe back to them.

Phoebe was used to seeing wreckages—she'd seen enough bodies pulled from crashed vehicles, but the sight of the helicopter, now a melted sculpture of metal, stopped her in her tracks. Literally.

It was enough to allow the police officer who'd been pursuing her since she'd skirted the crowd beyond the orange flags to catch up with her. And grab her roughly by the arm. 'You'll have to come with me.'

She did what any self-respecting woman would do in the circumstances and ignored him.

She glanced over her shoulder, looking for a landmark. 'This was where he was standing. Right here.' She tapped the ground with her foot as she talked to herself. The police officer stood beside her, seemingly with no idea what to do or how to deal with her. Her voice caught on a sob as she stood in Max's place, looking at the twisted, charred remains of the helicopter fifty metres away. She turned to the policeman. 'Have you seen him? Where is he? Where's Max?' Phoebe's voice tripped over itself as she visualised the scenario.

The helicopter had crashed, that was what had horrified Max. He would have seen it fall from the sky, would have had a clear view of its final descent over the cameraman's shoulder. She guessed she was standing roughly where Max had been. The crash would have happened in his direct line of sight, she judged as she surveyed the scene. She tried to quell her horror at the sight of the wreckage. If the helicopter had ended up that close, then—then—

She turned back to the officer and grabbed him by his arm. 'You have to help me find the man who was standing here when the chopper crashed. There was a reporter, a news camera. You have to help me.' Her voice shook with barely concealed panic and her blue eyes, brimming with unshed tears, appealed for assistance and compassion.

The young police officer looked completely bewildered by everything going on around him, not least of all by Phoebe, but he finally gathered his wits and replied, 'You think he was hurt?'

Phoebe gulped and nodded.

'Come with me,' he said, drawing her away from the chaos that was the destroyed helicopter and towards a cluster of media vehicles on the edge of the car park.

But the television crews couldn't give them any information, or none that Phoebe was after. The reporter and cameraman had both been taken to hospital suffering from shock and from minor cuts and abrasions sustained as the chopper had broken apart and showered the vicinity with debris. No one knew what had caused the crash and no one knew what had happened to the man who was being interviewed at the time.

Phoebe clamped one hand over her mouth. Two of the three people she was looking for had been taken to hospital so the chances were that Max had been, too. She felt nauseous but losing her composure now would get her nowhere. She saw an ambulance parked beside a fire engine and an enormous red bus. The paramedics would be able to tell her what she needed to know. She was one of them after all. She almost sprinted for the emergency vehicles, the young policeman trailing in her wake.

But all they could tell her was that the chopper pilot, by some miracle, had survived and he had been rushed to hospital along with the reporter and the cameraman. They could give her no information about anyone else.

That had to be good news, right? she asked herself more than once. But if Max *hadn't* been hurt, where was he?

She looked around the car park, straining to see into the darkness. 'How can a six-foot-two fireman disappear into thin air?' she muttered. 'He must be here somewhere.'

The police officer was staring at her. Did he think she was losing control? If so, he hadn't seen anything yet. She was just getting warmed up.

'You didn't say he was a fireman.'

Phoebe frowned. 'What?'

'You didn't tell me he was a fireman,' the policeman repeated. 'Follow me,' he said, and this time it was Phoebe trailing in his footsteps.

They were heading for the big red bus. The bus was brand-new and enormous. Its paintwork shone in the fluorescent lighting of the car park but its dark, tinted windows looked ominous. She could see the writing on its side now, naming it the Mobile Command Centre for the MFS.

She slowed her pace, letting the gap between her and the policeman widen. Her mouth was dry, her heartbeat rapid and her throat constricted by nerves. They were close to getting an answer but was it going to be one she wanted to hear?

The policeman had reached the bus and climbed the steps to the door, pausing at the top to check where Phoebe was. But Phoebe had come to a standstill. She couldn't make her legs move to cover those final few steps.

So she stood, fixed in place, as the door at the top of the steps opened, spilling light onto the black bitumen.

Then the light was obscured as the policeman went into the bus.

No, it wasn't someone going in, it was someone coming out.

And that same someone skirted past the junior policeman and took the steps in one stride. Someone tall and big and with a very familiar gait.

'Max?' she whispered.

And then he was in front of her.

He was real. He was alive. He was pulling her to him.

'Max!' Emotion took over and she threw her arms about his neck, pressed close against him, vaguely aware of the police officer still standing on the steps, obviously trying to work out what had just happened.

'Phoebe,' Max said when they'd finally stepped apart, both satisfied they weren't hallucinating and more than pleased to see each other. 'What are you doing here?'

Should she be worried at that? Briefly, she was, but there was nothing but joy in his eyes and he was beaming like it was Christmas, so she gave her doubts a hefty kick. 'I saw you being interviewed and then something happened and transmission was cut and we didn't know why.' She looked up at him. He had a cut on his cheekbone and her fingers stretched out, involuntarily, to touch his face.

Max reached up and pressed her fingers to his skin. 'You saw me being interviewed? In Adelaide? How did you get here so quickly?'

Phoebe frowned briefly before she realised Max had no idea she'd been in town. 'I'm staying at my friend Margot's. I'm here for her birthday. She drove me here. I had to come. I had to know you were OK.'

'You would have come if it was Ned? Or someone else you knew?'

'Of course.' Puzzled, she tried to read the expression in his eyes, which had clouded. 'Wouldn't you?'

'Yes, I guess I would.' Distracted by a vehicle coming past, he moved her to one side and said, 'Can we go somewhere? I'm off duty now, finally. A fresh batch of officers has finally arrived to relieve us and if I don't get to a shower soon I'll be declared the next state emergency.'

'Is there a hotel you're booked into or can you come back with me to Margot's? I need to talk to you, there are things I need to tell you, and—'

'There are things I need to say, too. Forget what I just said, I can't wait until I've had a shower.' He suddenly seemed impatient, distracted even. 'If you can stand being near a walking smoke stack, can we talk now?'

She wasn't sure what to make of that—not surprising when she'd been tossed from one emotion to another these last few hours. Was it her imagination or had he cooled since that first moment of relief and joy at seeing her? Had she just been a familiar face to him and nothing more?

Then he said, 'This might not be what you want to hear, but I need to say it.'

She stared blankly at him, no longer wanting to hear the words she knew were about to come. She would be losing the possibility of him all over again.

From the panicked look on her face, she didn't want to hear him out, but he'd make that mistake with her once before and the deed undone had gnawed away at his gut every day since. She might not want to listen but there was no way in hell he was letting her go without telling her what he'd come to realise.

'The only thought I had when I saw the chopper, was for you. I'd left you without telling—' Frustrated at his attempt to explain so much, he stopped and tried again. 'Just before I left to come here, I realised what you meant to me. I came out to the house to see if we could start again.'

'You came out? So I did hear you when Adam was there?'

'Yes.'

'But you left?'

'It seemed like you'd found what you wanted. But now, today, and at various times when the fires got a little much, I've been regretting that I didn't talk to you. Even if you have found what you want, I can't let you go without telling you how I feel. If there's the smallest chance that you *haven't* found what you need…'

She shook her head. 'I have found what I need.'

'I see.'

'No, I don't think you do.'

But he did, and it was killing him.

'I overheard you telling Adam it wasn't me you wanted. On reflection, I wondered if you'd said it was over not because you'd stopped caring but because you thought I didn't trust you. And then I thought maybe there was hope but a hurried phone call from the midst of bushfires wasn't the way to find out. In the end the only thing I knew for sure was that I *had* to know for sure. For a moment today I thought the last you'd hear of me was I'd been killed in a freak accident. And now, unbelievably, you're here.'

'Would you like to know why I came?'

'Yes, but before you tell me, there's one more

thing I have to say, just in case it makes any difference. I was wrong to blame you for not telling me every little thing there was to know about Adam. That's what I realised the day I left. I was about to ring Lisbette but then I realised there was nothing I needed to resolve there. Her behaviour had nothing to do with you and it was crazy to conclude that because one woman had betrayed me, the woman I wanted had to be a crystal-clear vessel, telling me her every thought. That's not what I want. The trust issue was my issue, it wasn't yours. In a relationship, if you trust, you don't second-guess all the time, and that's what I did to you. I was wrong.'

'But ever so right that I've found what I need.'

'You and Adam?' He'd been holding himself in check, steeling himself for this announcement. His jaw was locked with tension, his hands clenched by his sides. If he had to hear it, he wanted it short and sharp.

'Adam and I have come to a place of peace that we both needed.' And there it was. She wasn't looking regretful, or sorry for him, or anything he might have expected. She was looking, for want of a better word, radiant.

'But what *I* need,' she was saying, 'what I need for myself, in order to go forward, is standing right in front of me.'

It was with an effort that he refrained from glancing over his shoulder, so sure was he that she'd made her choice and it wasn't him.

It was only when she placed her fingers on his arm that he really started to understand that perhaps he still had reason to hope.

He was looking less strained now. Just. It would take more to clear his doubts after what he'd heard her saying to Adam. She reached out a hand and rested it on his forearm, willing him with her touch to hear what she was saying.

'It's you. You that I need.'

The doubts were lifting, she could see it in his face and in the way he unclenched his fists and loosened the tight bunching of his shoulder muscles. All she wanted was to step into the safe circle of his arms, but there was more she had to say.

'And I need to tell you one last thing, so there are no more secrets between us. I already knew how I felt about you when Adam asked me, but I thought I'd heard you at home. I couldn't bring myself to admit to wanting you, needing you, when I thought you didn't want me. And now I find out that if I had—'

'I would've come straight to you, pulled you out of his arms, told you I loved you.' His voice was rich with a joyous disbelief and longing that was as thrilling as any serenade. 'And then I would've kissed you, exactly like this…'

And he grabbed her to him in a single move so forceful it took her breath away and, she'd later admit to Margot, would have had her swooning with its power, if he hadn't been holding her as if he'd never let her go.

Much, much later, when he'd left her in no doubt she'd been a fool to have passed up the opportunity to be kissed like this days ago, they drew apart, just a little, to look at each other in wonder.

And then the sounds of the scene around them trickled back into consciousness and they became aware that once again Max was under the scrutiny of TV cameras, with a certain young police officer enjoying the role of keeping the reporters under control.

'Hell,' groaned Max as he realised they'd just overtaken the crashed chopper in newsworthiness.

Phoebe simply nestled into his side and beamed up at him. 'It's not every day a girl is wooed with national media coverage.'

He dropped a kiss on the tip of her nose and said, 'In that case, let's give you your fifteen minutes.' And he swung her out in front of him, folding his arms across her body, and held her tight as the cameras flashed.

'Max!' called one reporter, another perfectly coiffed blonde out of place in the chaos of the general scene. 'Our viewers have gone crazy with worry over you.' She was talking half to camera, half to Max, and from the blinking light atop the camera it seemed they were on air. 'We're so glad to see you weren't hurt, like Narelle.'

'The other reporter.' Max bent his head to whisper in Phoebe's ear as the woman chatted on to the camera.

'They all look the same to me.' She tilted her mouth up to whisper in his ear, confident the camera was trained on the hero of the moment and not some unknown TV reporter. 'Are you sure they're not cloned?'

'When Narelle asked you if you were single, women's hearts all over the country soared with hope.' Phoebe suppressed a giggle but couldn't stop the grin spreading across her face at what she was seeing—the reporter was pouting at Max. 'But it looks like we're seeing something unfold right here so if you don't mind, I'll put the question again. Max, are you single?'

Max looked at Phoebe.

Phoebe looked back. 'You said you loved me, right?'

'I did.'

'Then…' she fixed the camera with a smile as wide as her heart was full '…no, Max is not single.'

'And,' added Max, 'if everything goes as it should, I never will be again.' He caught the police officer's eye, the officer nodding to confirm he understood Max's subtle signal, and led Phoebe away from prying eyes.

'One last thing,' he said between kisses as they found a quieter spot where the police officer should be able to keep even a persistent reporter away, 'I need to get my head around.'

'Yes?'

'Is the love of my life a paramedic or a paediatrician?'

'Definitely a paramedic. Quitting medicine was

a bit of a knee-jerk reaction to everything else going on in my life at the time but now I can't imagine ever going back. I'm a different person now. I'm happy with this life, with my job, and now I have you, it all seems right.'

'What about your urge to escape to France to shell peas on doorsteps?'

'I can shell peas just as well here, although I wouldn't say no to a holiday there one day.' She leant her forehead against the rough fabric of his work jacket and the gesture grabbed at his heart. She couldn't have told him more clearly in words that she was savouring the feeling of belonging and of safety. 'It was like a talisman to hold on to, that image, of being somewhere that was so perfect nothing bad could happen, where life was simple and whole and good again.'

'It kept you going.' She nodded. 'And now?'

'Now I don't need something to hold on to. Nothing other than you,' she said as she slipped her arms about his torso. 'There's just one thing standing between me and complete satisfaction.'

'Yes?'

'I found out today the guy I'm in love with is a bona fide rock god.'

'And?' The smile that hadn't left his face since he'd kissed her was still flickering at the corner of his beautiful mouth.

'And he hasn't tried to get me into bed yet.'

He cleared his throat, and when he spoke, his voice had a growl in it. 'That's a problem?'

'I'm thinking it might be.' Max laughed and Phoebe automatically reached out to touch the place just under his jaw where he'd tilted his head back, distracted. 'And I think I've just found the only spot of clean skin on you.'

'Getting back to the problem you mentioned?' The growl in his voice had intensified to match the spark of humour shining in his eyes.

'There's going to be girls galore hurling themselves at you. I need to stake my claim.'

'And to think I had you pegged as a money-hungry brazen hussy when you're just a brazen hussy.'

And then he took her in his arms again, covering her mouth with his, leaving her in no doubt at all that, brazen hussy or not, she was all he either wanted or needed.

Later that night, Glen and Margot's living room overflowed with the laughter of four friends and the tinkle of champagne glasses as a series of toasts was made to all manner of happy events and future hopes. As Glen left to fetch more drinks, Phoebe stepped back to place a disc in the CD player, then lingered quietly, enjoying the picture of Max and Margot, the man she loved and the friend who'd never let go of her, deep in earnest discussion.

It would be some time before she could believe the miracle her friends and family had been praying for had happened. She wasn't the same woman she'd been three years ago but life hadn't bypassed her. She'd found her way back into the world of those who loved her, had found her way back to a place where she could start again. Older, yes, hopefully wiser, and with her love for her little boy as much a part of her as her breath. But the pain no longer consumed her so that it left no room for dreaming and loving and her heart now beat with dreams and hopes and the belief that she deserved to be loved. And most magical of all, she wasn't starting over by herself. The warm comfort of knowing she not only was entitled to be loved but actually *was* loved spread through her as Max walked over to her side, took her in his arms and pressed a soft kiss on her lips, before lifting his head to meet her gaze with his own.

Against all odds, she'd been given another chance.

'They're playing our song,' Max said as the CD player rotated to the new disc she'd inserted, and her soul soared as the opening strains of the music were overlaid with his rich, deep voice. His song, 'Coming Home'. 'I wrote this knowing what I needed was a place to start again, somewhere that could be home.' The corner of his full mouth lifted with the hint of a smile that unfurled her heart to its very limits. 'I didn't think I'd find it.'

'And did you?' Phoebe asked, knowing full well his response to her question would be another of his kisses, just to convince her he had found exactly what he'd needed. She raised her mouth to his, barely hearing his soft reply of 'I did,' before his lips found hers, igniting her senses with his touch, his scent, his taste. She melted into the delicious-ness of being in his arms, the aroma of champagne on his breath, the feel of his clean-shaven face, smooth against hers, the combined sensations so gorgeously heady it might have been a dream.

But it wasn't.

It was real. *Max* was real, as was the promise of a wonderful future together. 'Our song couldn't have a better title,' she whispered as his lips left hers as the song ended and he wrapped one strong arm about her shoulders, pulling her close. 'Who would have believed we'd be coming home to each other and starting over, together?' She nestled her head against his chest, silent for a moment as she felt the strong beat of his heart, marvelling that it seemed a physical affirmation of what she meant to him. 'Starting over from a place of love.'

'Starting, and more importantly…' he said as he caught her lips in another kiss, and then another, holding her tight to his chest until she could no longer tell where his heartbeat ended and hers began.

'Yes?' she prompted as they drew apart the tiniest bit, reluctant even for that much distance to be between them.

'Starting and, more importantly, going forward, the two of us together, without end.' The light in his eyes told her his dreams were every bit as rich and thrilling as her own. 'There's a wonderful life ahead of us, Phoebe.'

'And it starts right now?'

He shook his head. 'It started the first moment I saw you and it was clinched when I saw you in your running gear, all long, glistening limbs and flushed cheeks.'

'I'd swat you for that.' She laughed up at him. 'But that would mean I'd have to let you go.'

'You'll have to let me go soon anyway.' He nodded in the direction of their friends, who, Phoebe now saw, were standing with their arms slung about each other, beaming at them. 'We're under observation.'

'They look happy enough. It's what they've wanted for me after all. To come home to them, to have a new beginning,' whispered Phoebe. Max didn't speak, just chuckled softly in answer and pulled her against him for yet another demonstration of just how delicious new beginnings could be.

MEDICAL™

Large Print

Titles for the next six months…

February

THEIR MIRACLE BABY	Caroline Anderson
THE CHILDREN'S DOCTOR AND THE SINGLE MUM	Lilian Darcy
THE SPANISH DOCTOR'S LOVE-CHILD	Kate Hardy
PREGNANT NURSE, NEW-FOUND FAMILY	Lynne Marshall
HER VERY SPECIAL BOSS	Anne Fraser
THE GP'S MARRIAGE WISH	Judy Campbell

March

SHEIKH SURGEON CLAIMS HIS BRIDE	Josie Metcalfe
A PROPOSAL WORTH WAITING FOR	Lilian Darcy
A DOCTOR, A NURSE: A LITTLE MIRACLE	Carol Marinelli
TOP-NOTCH SURGEON, PREGNANT NURSE	Amy Andrews
A MOTHER FOR HIS SON	Gill Sanderson
THE PLAYBOY DOCTOR'S MARRIAGE PROPOSAL	Fiona Lowe

April

A BABY FOR EVE	Maggie Kingsley
MARRYING THE MILLIONAIRE DOCTOR	Alison Roberts
HIS VERY SPECIAL BRIDE	Joanna Neil
CITY SURGEON, OUTBACK BRIDE	Lucy Clark
A BOSS BEYOND COMPARE	Dianne Drake
THE EMERGENCY DOCTOR'S CHOSEN WIFE	Molly Evans

MILLS & BOON®
Pure reading pleasure™

0109 LP 2P P1 Medical

MEDICAL™

—⋀— *Large Print* —⋀—

May

DR DEVEREUX'S PROPOSAL	Margaret McDonagh
CHILDREN'S DOCTOR, MEANT-TO-BE WIFE	Meredith Webber
ITALIAN DOCTOR, SLEIGH-BELL BRIDE	Sarah Morgan
CHRISTMAS AT WILLOWMERE	Abigail Gordon
DR ROMANO'S CHRISTMAS BABY	Amy Andrews
THE DESERT SURGEON'S SECRET SON	Olivia Gates

June

A MUMMY FOR CHRISTMAS	Caroline Anderson
A BRIDE AND CHILD WORTH WAITING FOR	Marion Lennox
ONE MAGICAL CHRISTMAS	Carol Marinelli
THE GP'S MEANT-TO-BE BRIDE	Jennifer Taylor
THE ITALIAN SURGEON'S CHRISTMAS MIRACLE	Alison Roberts
CHILDREN'S DOCTOR, CHRISTMAS BRIDE	Lucy Clark

July

THE GREEK DOCTOR'S NEW-YEAR BABY	Kate Hardy
THE HEART SURGEON'S SECRET CHILD	Meredith Webber
THE MIDWIFE'S LITTLE MIRACLE	Fiona McArthur
THE SINGLE DAD'S NEW-YEAR BRIDE	Amy Andrews
THE WIFE HE'S BEEN WAITING FOR	Dianne Drake
POSH DOC CLAIMS HIS BRIDE	Anne Fraser

MILLS & BOON®
Pure reading pleasure™